Dick Fitswell

The Man in Quest of the Perfect Fit

by Jack Corbett

Published by Nirvana Publishing Company

1st Edition

by Jack Corbett

Artwork by Scott Waggoner
Printed by Createspace

For information address
Nirvana Publishing Company
4081 Grainleg Ave
Farmersville, IL 62533

http://www.alphapro.com
jack.corbett@gmail.com

Copyright March, 2012

ISBN--978-0-9647143-7-3

Other Books by Jack Corbett

Death on the Wild Side
Welcome to the Fun House

Introduction--Why did I create this monster?

Dick Fitswell is appalling. Overly endowed, at least part of Dick reaches epic proportions, which might be part of the reason he perceives women to be 2 dimensional objects who are worthy only of sexual exploitation. His quest is to find the perfect fit. Whereas other men might look for the perfect woman, a soulmate, or at least someone who can respect and enjoy them, Dick will have none of that, while viewing such men as being stupid and weak.

Dick's quest starts in a country Western Bar which leads him to a swinger's club, the Saint Louis Country Club, the Sun Valley Ski Resort, the Canadian wilderness just south of the Arctic Circle, to eventually becoming a minister of a church as he preys on the female members of the congregation. His journeys take him to Hong Kong, Bangkok, to the homeless areas of San Francisco to jobs working for American Online and Microsoft. But while he preys on the weaker sex with a vengeance Fitswell often receives more than he's bargained for with the last laugh usually being upon him.

This book is not for the fainthearted and above all keep it away from children. It is also not meant to be taken seriously. After all, I didn't want to create Fitswell in the first place. I was asked to do it by Jim Lilley who owned the *Wild Times*, which was a small St. Louis based adult magazine. I wanted to write a short story for Jim, a beautiful piece in my estimation called "Return to Visions", but Jim didn't seem to be very interested. So I called Alex up to ask her opinion. Alex was a stripper who was dancing in my favorite strip club in those days, Dollies Playhouse. Alex had been the very first person to ever read *Death on the Wild Side*, all 600 pages of it. I regarded Alex as a very bright woman who also just happened to be at least in my opinion a very fine poet, which is just one of her many bright sides her Dick Fitswell like customers never got to see. I did and I valued her opinion highly. So I told Alex, "Alex, I cannot write about this Dick Fitswell character and his overly large 18 inch appendage. It's just too pornographic. It's just not me. But if I want to get "Return to Visions" into the *Wild Times* I'm going to have to create this character for him."

I still remember Alex's reply. "You can do it Jack. You wrote some pretty earthy sections in *Death on the Wild Side*, and I should know because I'm the first person to have read it."

And so, I did it. I started to write my first Fitswell story which was first published in *The Wild Times* and was later published in *Xtreme Magazine* over on the East Coast. But from the very first story, I found the writing process to be extraordinary. I'd start to imagine all these bizarre episodes I'd put Fitswell into such as his getting his penis almost cremated by an electronic penis pump he was mistreating a Bangkok whore with and I'd just start laughing. Then I'd write a little more, and I'd break out laughing again. And so it went. I kept putting Dick into all these impossible scenarios, some of which he'd barely escape from with his life. I actually hated having to write the actual sex parts of my stories because I felt so uncomfortable doing it. Above all I really didn't like the kind of man I was writing about. So I really relished making him get his just deserts at the end of so many of my stories.

But through it all I started to love the character I had created in the same sense that one used to love Larry Hagman as JR Ewing. Jr Ewing in the television hit series *Dallas* was truly a very evil person. But Larry was able to pull off his characterization of JR with such aplomb that his audiences started to love J.R. And so it is with Fitwell. He's the kind of man who's easy to love to hate. He's like viewing a trainwreck that you really don't want to see, but you just can't help uncovering your eyes to watch it.

One might think that women in particular would hate reading about such a vile person as Dick Fitswell. But once I started to get underway with my character, many of my stripper friends would call me "Fitswell". They at least got the joke and found Fitswell to be terrifically funny.

I'd often sit at the bar in my favorite strip clubs working on my laptop creating the next Fitswell story while drinking with my dancer friends. Back in those days life was one big party for me that focused around the strip clubs. Whereas most other men had their neighborhood bars, I had my neighborhood strip clubs. Many of the girls would flit back and forth between their customers and me when I was in the clubs, and if they didn't have customers they'd sit with me as I played around with my laptop. At least three of the girls had done poetry on the side which I put up on my web site for them.

I can't even begin to count how many strippers would visit me at my apartment, or how many would go drinking with me when they were not working or had finished their shifts. They were, far more than the guys, my greatest friends about whom I have many great stories to tell but that's all going to have to wait on another book, either the one that comes after this one or the one after that.

My dancer friends and I would even do off the wall videos with me playing Fitswell, one of which still remains on my web site as I pretend to rape one of the girls in a hooded monks outfit. The girls egged me on, so whatever can be said about Fitswell, or about me, the writer, who created him, I cannot be accused of being anti woman or as a Fitswellian creature who gets his kicks out of abusing women. The women were my greatest fans and I was theirs as well. Back in those days they were my constant companions day in and day out, night after night. We drank together and we did a lot of laughing together. I could never have done Fitswell without their support and encouragement.

Dedication

To Alex--I wouldn't have done it until you told me I could do it.

And to Sahara, Angie, Skie, Angela, Jade, Angel, Selena, Marriah, and Satin and all of you girls from the Saint Louis Metro East clubs who were my constant loyal companions who encouraged me to write this book. And to Mary up in Michigan 400 miles away who constantly encouraged me to be my whacky off the wall self.

And to you, Big Howard, wherever you are now. Those were the best of times when you were manager at Dollies.

Dick Fitswell picks up a girl in a Country Western Bar

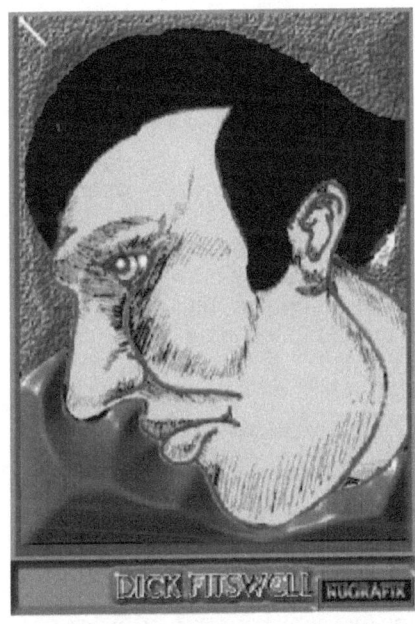

I'm the real man...the man on the prowl...looking, always searching for the perfect woman-not for brains or heart, but for the perfect fit. So listen up all you men who really want to score and see why I'm called Dick Fitswell. I've the man with the plan--- the man who makes it happen. Now, let me tell you about last night.

I hate country bars. Music's terrible. Conversation's piss poor. But they got women in this place and that's the bottom line. I need it bad tonight because last night was such a bummer. The girl was too damn short for me and it just didn't feel right with her clinging onto me...as she kept crying out, "I love you Dick I spy a tall blonde with great breasts. I can feel myself inside her already. She's mine. "She's not looking at me yet," I tell myself as I pull my shirt up a bit which exposes my magnificent chest. I tighten up my arms and watch the veins pop out in my forearms. I'm the shit. "How would you like to fall in love tonight?" I ask her.

Good line. I used to use--"Got a light?" but a lot of women don't like the smell of cigarettes on a man. Now I'll often get myself into a little sweat by exerting myself outside a bar before I walk in such as running around its parking lot a few times to give myself just the right amount of B.O. A lot of women love that smell. . Makes them think they're with a real man.

The band is playing "People looking for the wrong people in the wrong places" or something like that. Probably got the name wrong since I don't have a good memory. Killed too many brain cells from too much drinking but who gives a shit. Getting laid is what's important and it seems the more brain cells you kill the more women like you. Guess they just don't want anyone who's too smart.

We head out to the dance floor as her eyes melt into mine. Got her where I want her. Pulling her close to my chest she puts both arms around my neck as I feel those wondrous breasts jabbing into my well developed pecs."You have great breasts," I tell her. Undo a few buttons." She undoes her buttons as I rip my shirt open. You can often tell the age of a woman by her breasts if you know what you are doing. It's like counting the rings in a tree trunk. She's only around 21. Her nipples tell me that.

I"ve got a huge erection. Now a lot of you guys are going to pull away, embarrassed by that protruding thing between your legs, Don't make that mistake. And here's another one you can't afford to make. Don't come in your pants. Especially if you are wearing light colored pants or shorts. And don't wear boxer shorts. Wear tightly fitting jockey shorts. I remember back in college making out with a girl when I took her back to her dorm. Got too damn excited and coming into my pants I felt my semen dribbling down my leg. Then I looked down at her feet which were just inside mine and saw my sperm collecting on the tops of her feet.

"I want you real bad," I whisper into her ear back at the bar. She wants to have another drink but I've got the perfect line for that which I've been rehearsing for weeks. "Drinking will spoil everything." "I want to feel every nerve in my body wanting you. Don't want to miss your scent. This is our first time and I don't want it to be the last time. (here I lied because the next night I knew I'd probably be picking up someone else). For the first time in weeks I feel really alive. I want you. Let's blow this pop stand."

12

It worked. I took her to my car outside. I reach into the glove box and pull out a small bottle of pills. The girl notices me swallowing one of them, looks at me, then asks, "What are those?" "Mild pain killers," I tell her. She probably thinks they are drugs and wants some. An antidepressant, they don't take away a man's sex drive, toning it down just the right amount. Gives me great staying power and they always keep me from coming in my pants. The problem is they take away from your initial hard on and you want the girl to feel your shaft up against her. You want her to feel it big and pulsating so there's no mistake what you are planning with her. So if you ever find any peter downer pills don't take them until an hour before you screw her.

Hand in hand we go into the bedroom. And that's another thing, when you've made the sale don't blow it. Fuck her as soon as you can. There will be plenty of time for talking later. Like after you've come six times and your rod feels spent and broken. The blonde takes her clothes off. I've got mine off in twenty seconds leaving my socks on. I mean.....who needs to take his socks off when the moment of truth arrives. She grabs my penis as soon as she sees me naked, she sits on the bed with her nipples hard just thinking about what's to come------me. And pulls me towards her, her eyes beckoning. It hurts and I have no choice. She's got a good grip on my shaft and I keep moving towards her. No choice at all since I will be disemboweled if I don't move in her direction.

She won't let go. Won't stop. I'd scream with the pain but I'm too much man for that. Then she lies down and spreads her legs pulling me by my organ right on top of her. Sticks it right in and starts squirming on the bed. "She's done this many times before, " I tell myself and the moment is so exhilarating with both the pain and the pleasure and the feel of her nipples throbbing in my chest so acute that if I were any other man I'd come as soon as I entered her. But I'm Dick Fitswell and I've got my ace in the hole working inside me. The Peter Downer pills.

"I'm not going to come," I'm thinking. She just doesn't know about those pills." She's got my shaft still between her fingers pressing tightly as it swells up. The pain is exquisite as she puts it inside her. Her legs go up around me as she holds herself tight.

13

"Come Dick," she pants, begging for it." But I'm Dick Fitswell and my mind has suddenly become philosophical. I am not about to come. "How does this one feel?" I ask myself. "Wet and definitely loose. Not as tight as many I've had. Exciting gal. I'd be her slave if it wasn't for those pills. I would do anything she'd want me to do. If she wanted to ride me around the room like someone riding a dog, I'd submit to it----just to come in her mouth. She could whip me and have me bark. I'd do it." I had fucked lots of girls. Hundreds of them and I knew her kind. She wants to be in control. Time to turn the tables. Whimpering now-----"Why haven't you come yet," she just didn't get it. My turn.

"Hey baby. You have just started the night of your life. Do you know my full name?" I asked. "Dick," she screamed. Come into me. I want to feel your juices."

"Not on your life. Or at least not just yet. My full name is Dick Fitswell. And I want to really think about you, my being inside you. Let's feel this out together. See that bottle of tequila on the stand behind you? Keep me inside you and pour us two glasses of tequila. Never mind that there's no ice."

Somehow she was able to do it and with me still inside her. I felt her put the glass to my mouth as I started to drink the fiery liquid. Savoring the moment I calmly thought about how she fit around my shaft. "Not tight enough." I have to keep searching for the perfect fit. Normally I would have liked her, but I'm on the eternal quest and liking has nothing to do with it. It's all a matter of mechanics. Like two gears meshing together. Still.........she was there...so it was time to have fun. I'll worry about the next girl tomorrow night.

"I wish you would come," she replied.

"I will. But first you have to do exactly what I ask you to do."

Her nipples were long and hard as I lifted up my head to take one of them into my mouth. I would have come right there "They are perfect," I said to myself as it tightened up against my tongue. Gently sucking, then biting hard into it. Just enough to make her

14

hurt until I heard her scream out...."Stop. You are hurting me." .
Thrusting violently into her I watched her body jerk each time I
pumped her. Her voice became a refrain, calling out to me----
"Give it to me, baby. I want it deeper. Come into me."

"I can't come until you promise me something, then I'll give you
what you want."

"Anything. I'll do anything," she screamed at me.

"Tomorrow night I want you to meet me at that bar again. Bring
the most beautiful girl you know. Tomorrow night I want to fuck
you both."

"Don't you want me?" she yelled.

"Sure I do," I lied. "More than anything in this world. But you
won't believe how good it will be tomorrow night."

"Do I have to?" she pleaded.

"If you want me to come," you have to.

"Okay. Now give it to me. Give it to me right now."

My strokes now became slow and easy as I savored her wetness.
I closed my eyes and started thinking about someone else. The
perfect fit I had yet to meet. That is my mecca. My quest and
when I find it I'll be in love.. With each thrust I became more like
a machine. Riding her with my legs around her I shot into her----
spasm after spasm----jetting right into her consciousness. In my
head her screams just a background noise dimly heard, calling out
to me It was only when I finished that I asked her, "What's your
name?" "Gloria," she replied. "Good name," I answered. Just want
to know who I'm fucking." Then I took her home. Let her walk
herself to the door as I sat behind the wheel. "They don't like
gentlemen anymore," I reflected calmly as I watched her let
herself into her apartment. Won't respect a man who's a
gentleman.

Dick Fitswell at the Swinger's Club

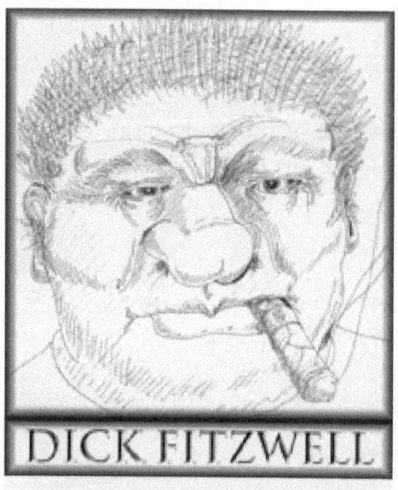

DICK FITZWELL

"ANYBODY KNOW A GOOD INTERN?"

Dick Fitswell ten years after this book was written

That last Cement mixer got me. The last thing I remember was swirling the shot of tequila around in my mouth with the lime shot, shaking my head violently then swallowing. I immediately passed out.

I found myself waking up to two women groping me between my legs. Six months ago I became a regular at the "If it works fix it Haven for Swingers". Made it a habit to go five nights a week and it was only three months ago that they changed the place from "The Erection Zone" to the new name, which probably had much to do with me. I'm the only Dick Fitswell, the man in search for the perfect fit, and I have the record for screwing the most women in 6476 successfully completed sexual encounters.

"Remember us from last week?" the willowy blonde breathed into my neck. My balls ached dully until I looked at her, taking in her slender waist and long legs as my appendage sprung to its full 18 inches .

"We are sisters," said the other one, as she climbed onto my face. "We wanted you so bad last week but you were all tired out.

I loved the place at first sight since I have a deep respect for good old no nonsense fucking. Here every woman with two legs is a target. Best part of it is you just point your dick in the right direction and you are rewarded by immediate penetration. Still.....I have not found what I've been looking for__the right tension and sucking action on my cock to achieve the perfect orgasm I've dreamed about.

"I'll fuck him while you slide yourself onto his face," the blonde said, as my penis slid into her opening. Her dampness soothed my swelled up member which had already seen three orgasms in just two hours. I lay there with closed eyes waiting to open them to her pretty face pushed close to my head, just before her tongue entered my mouth. As I thrust upwards into her I could feel her shudder. "Oh Gawd," I told myself. "I can feel her quiver around my penis. She's the best."

I waited for her lips to meet mine. Confident I could time my orgasm perfectly with the blonde, I started to feel something soggy around my mouth. Opening my eyes I could see the fat ass of her sister bearing down on me. Subconsciously I tried to pull back but my head was firmly rooted to the couch I lay on. Feeling her weight around my face as my tongue took a mind of its own I started to concentrate on the blonde.

Thrusting vigorously as she lay on top of me, the blonde started to lose control and I can't fault her for that since I"m Dick Fitswell, the man every woman wants. Her opening, at first tight, became looser as her juices started to flow. By now all I could think about was her sister, who must have weighed around one hundred and eighty.

Her sister, a brunette with a hawk shaped nose, was hunkering down on me as I tried to move my head for a breath of fresh air. Suddenly the blonde pulled off me...she had been riding me face to face...but the brunette had gotten in the way and spoiled it all. I felt the blonde kneel down over my dick and this time I knew I was entering her from the rear. Once again I felt that exquisite tightness and knew I was in love. I wanted to call out to her...to tell her I loved her and jerked my head upwards only to feel my tongue going more deeply into her sister. Which was about as sensual as sticking it in a large tank of diesel fuel. By this time my face was buried deeply into that furry thing that now resembled a grizzly bear and I once again started to lose that perfect meeting

17

of bodily parts with the woman I now craved more than any other.

"Come Dick. I"m coming. Spurt into me," I dimly heard the blonde call out to me but the insulation around my face was too thick and her words became lost in imagined grunts and groans in an Alaskan swamp where I was being thrust down into the mire by a female grizzly. It was then that I lost the thing that was most precious to me. My erection. It was the first time it had ever happened to me.

"Dick....I've come twice," the blonde shouted. "What's wrong with you?"

"I've come all over his face three times, "the hefty brunette added. "We're done Julie. Let's find a couple more guys."

That perfect moment that would have etched itself permanently in time had the blonde and I been alone became the worst time of my life. I was sure that men who had both legs shot off in battle couldn't have had it worse than me. The two women climbed off me and started to walk away. I jumped up and caught up with the pretty blonde.

"Let's you and I get together. Just you and me," I whispered into her ear.

"Sorry.........I only fuck guys when my sister's doing it with me," she replied as she moved away from me.

"No more Mr Nice Guy", I told myself. "I'm tired of being a gentleman and fucking every woman who wants me. For me the unspoken rules of etiquette for the "If it works fix it Haven for Swingers" was that I had to take on all comers. "There's just too many ugly bitches in the place. Now how in the hell will I ever find the perfect fit when I'm screwing everything that walks? I will just have to become more selective. I'm blowing this place and I'm never going to darken its doorway again with my carcass."

I walked out the door and never looked back. And the worse part of it was.........I hadn't even had an orgasm with the blonde. "But they can't keep Dick Fitswell down for long." Suddenly I came up with a new plan. I would have to be more discerning about who I'm sticking my penis into. From now on I will be going to places where the women will be much more attractive and where I can jump them one at a time. "Strip clubs. That's the scene for Dick Fitswell. Only in a strip club will I meet my soul mate--I mean perfect fit. Swinging sucks"

Dick Fitswell at the Strip Club

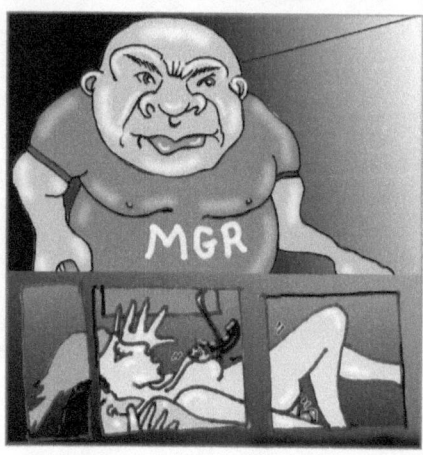

It is me again. Dick Fitswell looking for the perfect fit and this time I'm doing it right, watching all the dancers come into the strip club as the day shift is being replaced by the night girls. I watch them come into the club's parking lot, sometimes in a cab, but usually driven by someone else, often their boyfriends. And then I see her, a brunette with a tight butt who will become the object of my dreams tonight--if she's lucky. The car has just pulled up next to mine and I can hear her boyfriend's last words to her-------"Now bring lots of money to me tonight Susan. I want you to crunch a lot of laps." I feel sorry for her as soon as I hear those words come out of the leech's mouth so tonight I will try to make her mine.

There is no time to lose. I have to get to her before she gets a lot of attention from the other customers. Then I see it and can't believe it as a new plan unfolds in my alcohol addled mind. A phone booth. Awfully convenient place for ole Dick to get his first piece of the night. Thanking my boy scout training I reach into my pocket for the Swiss Army knife I always carry. I almost hate myself for doing it but "there's no other way" I tell myself as I open the blade and cut into the meat of my hand, not too deep, but just enough to let the blood flow like a fine wine. I grab a napkin from my little table and jam it over my injured hand. After a few seconds my blood starts to seep through for just the right effect.

Susan's sitting over at the bar. Probably still seething from her pimp boyfriend asking her to bring home lots of money so he can sit on his fat ass. She's right where I want her. Holding the napkin against my injured hand I walk up to her asking "Can you please help me make a phone call? Just cut my hand and I need help in that phone booth with the quarters."

"Sure," she replies, as she gets up from her bar stool.

I enter the phone booth first and make a great show of trying to pick up the receiver, almost dropping it as I pretend to wince with pain. "It hurts," I tell her but that doesn't matter. I just don't want that napkin to come off and get my blood all over the place. Come in and help me." The booth is crowded with two of us in it. I don't know what it is but the sight of blood either scares a woman or gets her sexually aroused. I can already feel her breasts stiffen in her excitement from being close to me.

"The quarters...they are in my front pocket. Reach in an get them," I tell her. "Don't want to get blood all over my pants. I have an erection waiting for her as she sticks her fingers in my pants and starts feeling around for the quarters. I have an eighteen inch slong and by now she's got ten inches of it firmly in her grasp. Her fingers open and close excitedly around my dick which makes me become even more erect. I know I've got her now since she's already forgotten about the quarters. Pulling my pants down I give her a good look at it. As if in a trance she kneels beneath me and starts to suck it.

This is total bullshit. A blow job at time like this? I'm Fitswell and I am interested in one thing...the perfect fit. She pulls her g string aside for me as I enter her seconds later. Then the idea hits me. "I"m fucking you in the ass," I tell her.

"Don't do that!" she says. "We don't have any vaseline."

"Who needs that shit. Watch me."

I spit into my right hand, the one that's not wounded. A lot of spit comes out of my mouth. Then I rub it into her orifice. I can feel

21

her heat as she becomes titillated from the wetness . But it's more likely the manliness of my spitting into my hand then rubbing it into her. Gets them every time.. She gasps in pain as I enter her and yells out to me...."Stop."

"No, better a Dick up the ass than a leech in the house," I reply knowing she will forget all about that boyfriend of hers once she gets my full charge.

Thrusting right into her I feel the tightness clamp around my my dick. She's in ecstasy and white hot as she alternates between shoving herself tightly against me and trying to pull away as she breaks out screaming. I ignore her screams knowing it's her way of telling me she loves me.

How can I ever forget that threshing around? She starts to climb the wall of the booth trying to escape from the inevitable...the infamous Fitswell cattle prod. Suddenly the phone booth starts to teeter, then crashes to the floor. She's knocked the damn thing over. How embarrassing. Then I see that it's far worse than that. The booth is upside down with the door on the bottom. We can't get out. Amazingly, I haven't pulled out of her.

I hear men running up to the booth but it's too late now. I have her head against the door of the phone booth which is now its bottom and keep pumping her. I hear a man's voice yelling at us------"Get the fuck out of there." But I'm in no mood to argue cause I'm busy now. Jamming it deeper I start coming, in little spurts at first, then I start injecting tons of stuff up her ass. I yell out to the guy....."Can't you see I'm fucking. When I'm done you can help me get out of this crate."

"Son of a bitch. It's the manager," I tell Susan. "Sorry that he has to spoil the magic moment for you." The manager needs all the help he can get. He's got the doorman and two customers with him. The four men lift the booth off the floor and set it upright so we can get out the door.

Now if there's one thing I am, it's being polite. So I tell them all...."Thanks guys. I think I'll even stay for a few more beers. "

"No, you're not," the manager tells me as he points his finger at my face. "Leave my club and leave it now. You are barred buddy and don't you ever come back." Then he turns to Susan. "You are fired girl. Start packing. Hit the streets bitch because a street whore is all you ever will amount to."

"Damn ungrateful bastard." I could have been his best customer. I was so pissed that I took Susan home with me. Fucked her three times then sent her home in a cab. From now on I'm staying out of clubs for at least a few months. She's bound to be at another club soon and will probably want to move in with me. Who wouldn't with a leech like she's got with her now. Great looking gal but dammit she just didn't fit me well enough. Have to move on and with luck I'll never see her again.

Dick Fitswell at the St Louis Country Club

It was that fake id that got me into the St Louis Country Club, the ID belonging to a guy I had just met named Elixir McDonald. I had beaten him in a game of pool and since he had run out of money he lent me his ID if I promised to return it. Borrowing a set of clubs from my neighbor I headed out onto the golf course not having the slightest idea of how to play. The course was 18 holes and I sure as hell wasn't there to play golf. I was there to pick up a high society woman. Elixir must have been a guy like me since they let me right onto the course when I produced his membership card. Sure as hell didn't play much golf, I thought, since they didn't seem to know that I wasn't Elixir.

I saw a bunch of guys teeing off at the first hole and watched what they were doing. Until now I thought a club was something you used to beat someone's brains in when you felt like picking a fight. After watching a few golfers tee off I knew what I had to do. I waited my turn, teed off, then went out to pick up my ball fifty feet away. It was not a good shot but I couldn't care less. I had more important things on my mind. I kept an eye out to make sure no one was watching and carried my ball to the 18th hole. There I waited for the foursome ahead of me to finish, then I put my ball six inches from the hole and putted it in.

It was time for the clubhouse bar and finding a woman to pick up. I had never seen the bartender before but he came up to me as if he had known me all his life. It was then that I noticed the tall brunette sitting down at the bar with three of her friends. "What can I get you?" the bartender asked.

"How about a double shot of tequila, I replied raising my voice just high enough that the women could hear me. "I had a terrible game today, and I need something that will make me forget it."

"Hate to hear it, " the bartender replied, his voice sympathetic, but I knew he was conning me. "After all, why should he give a shit about how my game went?" I decided two could play the con game.

"74 for the 18 holes I replied. Terrible game."

The brunette heard me loud and clear. 74 for 18 holes is 37 for nine which is an average of 4 per hole. Now that's outstanding. In her middle thirties, she looked like she had been around the course a few times and knew what a 74 stood for. She probably figured me for one of the top pros in the U.S. and might even approach me for free golf lessons. I must have figured right. She said loudly--------"A 74 is bad? You can give me lessons anytime."

I looked at her with that special look I had been practicing in the mirror lately----a look of pain and surprise. Then answered----"I don't think I am good enough to give you lessons but I'll buy you a drink."

Not having a moment to lose I was over there in a heartbeat. As soon as I had paid for the drinks I asked, "Can you show me around the club house? I'm new here. Just moved to St Louis."

She had obviously had a few. I like them like that since they don't know what they are doing. I knew I had to get her right away or risk losing her and I could not afford that since she was long legged and trim. Hopefully she would be tight. She showed me all around the club house. Then I asked where the men's room was. After she led me to the men's room I asked her to wait for me at the door promising I'd be quick. But I"m Dick Fitswell, the man with the plan and I had it all figured out. I was in the men's room for only twenty seconds before I came out with just the right amount of surprise on my face...another look I had carefully rehearsed in front of the mirror.

"Something's wrong with the plumbing," I told her. There's water all over the floor. Can you do me a favor?"

"Sure. Just tell me what," she replied.

"Go in the ladies room with me and make sure no one comes in. I promise I won't take long, " but what I really meant was..."I won't take long to fuck you."

We went in there together but I knew what she really wanted. Taking her by the hand I took her to the closest stall, bent her over, and pulled her shorts up to her knees. She was one of those rich bitches. Otherwise she sure as hell wouldn't be at the St Louis Country Club. And I knew from experience that most rich bitches liked it in the ass. I had reasoned it was because they were so used to getting their way that having a man abuse them that way was a sexual turn on since it did not fall in with their life's experiences. I started in on her and was glad I didn't have any Vaseline to spoil it for her. Right off she started panting, then screamed in pain as I rammed deep into her. But I am Dick Fitswell, the man after the perfect fit and assholes just don't cut it with me. It's just the means to the other end.

I pulled out of her as she gave a deep gasp, turned her around forcibly just to show her who was boss and bent her over the toilet before I entered her from the front. Suddenly we heard women's voices inside the ladies room. It was her friends. "There's a man in the stall," one of them yelled. Now that's when I really get turned on...when other people are around while I'm fucking somebody. I could hear the other women shouting as I rammed deeply into her. I laughed to myself when her head hit the toilet. It was an accident and she didn't knock herself out but I noted to myself with satisfaction that she would probably have a headache later on. But the other women kept shouting which made me thrust more violently, losing all sensation of what should have been a tight fit around my dick. It was the other women who were the turn on. Suddenly I lost it and started to come as I rocked her up against the stool.

We walked out of the stall hand in hand as her three friends stood just inside the door with those haughty looks on their faces only the rich seem to get just right. I would have taken it as a sign of disapproval with our behavior but I knew better. They were just mad that I wasn't fucking them instead. As we came up to them I pulled out four business cards and handed one to each woman.

"I'm having a party this Friday night at 8 PM, and I would be honored if all four of you can be there." But I was lying. I had other plans for Friday night. One of my buddies had just gotten a job as a bartender at a biker bar and I had promised myself to fuck a biker woman that night. As the woman and I walked out the door, my mind was off of her already, transporting itself to thoughts of a tall blonde riding a Harley with her breasts heaving heavily in the wind.

Dick Fitswell at the Biker Bar

Afraid to go into a biker bar? Not if you are Dick Fitswell, the man out for the perfect fit, and I'm the man out for the perfect lay. I will do anything to nail the right piece down and I don't give a damn where I have to go to find the object of my quest. I walked into the biker bar, confident and ready as every man in the place gave me the once over with his eyes. And then I saw her-----a tall ravishing blonde, with a tight ass and breasts that jutted out into sharp little points--the kind of breasts that makes a grown man want to cry. God...did I want her.

Being meek in a biker bar with all those Harleys and bikers just doesn't get it and being too cocky can get a man killed. I ordered everyone in the place a drink----including the bartender. Especially the bartender. One guy, a gruff long haired freak with a beard who appeared to be the leader immediately asked me right after he tasted his beer-----"This stuff tastes funny. I don't know if I want to drink it."

"It should taste funny," I told the man. "It's Samuel Adams Cherry Wheat. Brought my own stock in." which I later found was a mistake to tell him. But at the time I was supremely confident. I had just poisoned everyone in the place. It had been easy to pull off since the owner was an independent kind of guy much like his clientele most of whom rode Harleys to the bar. I had come in earlier with several cases of Samuel Adams and told the owner that I had friends coming in and I wanted to make a special occasion of that evening for my friends. Whole thing went like duck soup. I had removed the cap off each bottle and put fresh caps back on using a special tool I often used while brewing my own. But first I dumped just the right amount of chloral hydrate in each bottle-----which was just enough to put to sleep four German shepherds.

What's good enough for German Shepherds is good enough for bikers the way I've got it figured. Make their tattoos stand out as they go down under. And make no mistake....Samuel Adams is damn good stuff. Every biker in the place took some. Their women too so I soon had the object of my hard on just where I wanted her. Within an hour everyone in the place had either fallen asleep or wasn't worth a shit----walking around like zombies in search of their names. Even the bartender passed out. "Good work, Fitswell," I told myself. "You are a flipping genius."

I found the blonde passed out on a bar stool and scooped her up in my arms. I heard a voice of protest from one of the bikers who had not passed out. "Shut up, Mother fucker," I told the man. Stumbling up to me, his mind turned to jello by the chloral hydrate, he took a swing which I easily ducked because I'm Dick Fitswell the man who's always got the plan. I decided to put him out of his misery and shot a right cross to his chin. "Curtains brother," I taunted him as he crashed to the floor. "Dream of sheep."

And speaking of sheep, it was time to get laid. I took the blonde out to my Corvette and laid her in the passenger seat. Then I clicked the radar detector on and drove home at over 100 miles per hour. She was still asleep when I carried her into my bedroom, laid her on my bed, and took her clothes off. She was snoring when I crunched on top of her, spread her legs wide open with my hands, and plunged my dick into her.

She woke up right after my twentieth thrust. Smiling at me out of limbo land, she said....."Thanks for rescuing me. You are really a gentleman." That got me laughing so hard--I immediately lost my erection. But I'm Fitswell the man up to any occasion so I jumped off of her and kneeled over her with my knees just outside her shapely legs.

"Get me hard, " I ordered as I stuck my hot rod into her mouth. I didn't have to tell her twice. Like a cowed dog she took the whole thing into her mouth and started sucking. "That's enough, " I told her. Turn over while I fuck you from the rear." Still dopey from the choral hydrate she turned over onto her belly as I rammed my shaft deep inside her. But I think I outsmarted myself. Because she sure was loose. Must be that choral hydrate ", I told myself.

"Relaxes the muscles too much and one just can't get a tight fit anymore. I've had ten year old work boots that fit tighter than that even after my size tens ballooned up to twelve's'.

Disgusted after I came I called a cab because she sure wasn't fun enough to fuck her in the car while driving her home. I fell asleep ten minutes after I heard her walk outside. Would have taken her to the door but she's a biker girl and biker girls don't respect gentlemen.

I got up early the next morning, made myself a pot of coffee, lit a cigarette, then went outside to admire my new Vette---------my chariot to many future orgasms. But it was gone. Vanished. The Vette was nowhere to be seen. I went out to where I had parked it hoping that somehow it would reappear. Instead I found a little red tricycle . On the seat I found a note which read--"Have fun on your future dates. Your friends from last night."

I had underestimated the blonde. Damn bitch had snitched on me. Me. Dick Fitswell." Now how could she do something like that after everything I had done for her? She had obviously carefully noted my address and car as she cabbed it home. "One can never trust a woman. I need a vacation. Been getting into a rut. Next week I'm going skiing."

Dick Fitswell goes skiing at Sun Valley, Idaho

"No more biker women for me or strippers. I deserve a vacation. After all, I'm Dick Fitswell, and I haven't found the perfect fit yet. It's Sun Valley for me, and if it was good enough for Hemingway and Gary Cooper it might be good enough for me and my 18 inch dick, which from now on I am going to call Caesar. After all, I have come to bury Caesar not to praise him. I'll just have to see what the women can do for me in this icebox."

"I was just shot down. By four girls in a row. I can't believe it. But it helps to know how to ski. I fell down seventeen times on the first run down Baldy yesterday. No one was impressed. But I got a plan. Yesterday people were laughing at me. Today I will have the best looking babe I can find feeling sorry for me. Don't believe me? Just watch. And that, my friends, is going to get me laid."

****

Dressed to the gills in fluorescent red ski bibs Dick Fitswell edged into the line at the chair lift. A tall shapely blonde wearing one of the tightest ski bibs ever seen on Baldy was in line, hatless, her long hair hanging down her neck. Fitswell shuffled next to her and called out: "Single". The blonde moved to the side letting Dick pull up next to her. It is customary to yell out single if you are in the chair lift line and don't have someone to ride up the mountain with you. With rare exception the other "single skier" moves aside to let the newcomer pole up. In twos and threes skiers pole up to the pickup spot where the first pair or threesome in line quickly sit in the double or triple chairs which scoops them onto cable borne ascents to the summit. Today was unusual since Sun Valley was having professional races in which the top skiers in the U.S. were competing.

One doesn"t have to wait long in chair lift lines at Sun Valley, which is one of many reasons why the resort commands some of the steepest lift ticket prices in the United States. Dick trudged along the snow slowly, his face showing pain as he shuffled along. They were soon standing in their skis where the chairs come closest to ground level, positioning themselves so the next chair would gently hit them in their butts and whisk them into the air. Moments later the two were aloft, on their way to the top, the snow twenty-five feet below them.

"Where are you from?" Dick asked the pretty woman sitting next to him.

"Montana. I come here a couple times a year."

"I'm from Wyoming," Fitswell lied. "Lived in Jackson Hole, Wyoming all my life," he lied a second time. "I like it since it has some of the toughest skiing in the country," he lied a third time. Which was partially true since Jackson Hole is nearly infamous for having some outrageously tough runs. Where Dick was lying is that he had never come within a hundred miles of Jackson Hole since the time he had gone to Yellowstone National Park where he had admired the geyser erupting hot lava while imagining himself to be the son of Ole Yellowstone in human form.

"You must be a great skier then, " the woman replied.

"I'm one of the racers competing for the Sun Valley cup," Fitswell lied a fourth time. "But I just got hurt. I hope I didn't break my leg."

"How did that happen?"

"Ran into a tree. I had the best time by far but I just lost it. I should get off this mountain and see a doctor."

"They will just put you in a chair at the top and have it take you down the mountain," the woman said. "But what are you going to do when you get off this mountain?"

"Getting down is not the problem. It's getting to the doctor afterwards. I don't have anyone to get me to the hospital."

"I'll help get you off the mountain and to the hospital," she replied.

Everything about Sun Valley is first class and getting Fitswell off Baldy was no exception. The attendants were very helpful, putting

Dick and his new escort on a chair heading down the mountain. They found a bus waiting for them at the bottom. The woman helped Dick put his skis in the rack on the side of the bus and the two boarded, as Dick made a big show of limping painfully to his seat. They got off close to the woman's condo where she helped him limp the rest of the way to her front wheel drive Saab. At the hospital the blonde helped Dick walk to the emergency room.

"This is going to take awhile, Dick told the woman, as he handed a fake insurance card to the receptionist. "Why don't we meet for dinner tonight?"

"Where?" the woman asked.

"How about the Christiana Restaurant?   It's where Ernest Hemingway had his last meal before he shot himself. We can meet at seven?"

"I'll be there," said the woman. But I can wait for you and give you a ride back."

"I might be awhile. You know how these things go. I'll just cab it back. My condo's next to the Christiana."

******

Here comes the tricky part. She' s gone and here I am in a little room waiting for the doctor to see me. Gotta find one of those walkers--one of those removable casts-- before the doctor comes in and spoils everything. I think I'll just look around this place, Dick Fitswell remarked to himself.

If there's one thing Dick Fitswell is good at, it's walking around looking important. He soon found a nurse and asked her--"Where do you keep those removable casts? I'm here representing the company that makes them and I want to make sure that your casts are not defective."

"I'll find one," the nurse replied.

Minutes later Dick was wearing a blue portable walker as he limped out of the hospital and took a cab to his condo.

****

"That was a great meal, Dick. The lamb was perfect. Too bad you broke your leg and have to strap on that blue walker. I know how much it means not being able to rejoin the competition. But there's always next year."

"Winning the Sun Valley cup has always been my dream and I had it in the bag. I was really burning up the slopes. My turns were flawless. I skied so close to the flags that I could feel them massage my chest through my bibs. And then I hit that icy spot and spun out into the trees. Let's have another margarita," Dick said matter of factly, knowing too only too well that playing too much the braggart just didn't get it with most women.

Two margaritas later the woman was visibly intoxicated. Dick Fitswell paid the bill and ambled out of the restaurant onto the snow covered sidewalk, as the blond took his arm to keep him from slipping.

I can take her to my condo and fuck her there, Fitswell said to himself, *but that's too easy. I have looked long and hard for the perfect fit and that's just not going to get it. She's got a great bod but I've had plenty of those and I've always wound up disappointed.*

The condos were close together surrounded by evergreens. As they came up to his building, Dick took the blonde by the arm and said...."Let's go over into those trees. I want to show you something", as he chuckled to himself....*Yeah baby I'm showing you something. My 18 inch schlong.*

Back in the trees next to his building, he said to her: "You've been so helpful. I rarely find a woman like you and you are so beautiful. I want to savor this moment and never forget it. The air is cold but this setting is so perfect, like a fairy tale land. I want you to stay here with me for a few minutes before we go inside." Her face looked up into his eyes as he pulled her close to him as and started to kiss her gently on the lips.

Need to get her lying down in the snow, he told himself. *I've been reading in Studman magazine about how a woman's genitals*

34

contract if you can just get her cold enough and that makes her fit tighter. It just might work.

He kissed her feverishly, then pulled back and looked her thoughtfully in the face which was pretty damn tough because aside from fucking her all he wanted to do was to laugh. "I am going to ask you something I've never asked a woman before. I've always wondered if I could make it in the snow with a woman but I've never been with the right woman before. It has to be cold lying in the snow. That has to detract from a guy's sexual pleasure. Has to make a man's penis shrink (Yeah, I hope it makes your pussy shrink, he told himself). Only a very special woman can keep a man completely tuned in--completely immersed in her both physically and mentally. I think you are that woman. I want you."

"Do you really think we should try that? Sounds sort of painful to me."

"I think we owe it to ourselves to try it. If we don't we will always wonder and secretly hate ourselves for not doing it."

"You have a broken leg. I'd better be on top then."

Not on your life, Dick thought. *You are going to freeze your ass off, not me. I need to get myself out of this one.*

"Not a good idea," Dick replied. If you are on top you might make a sudden move that could hurt my leg but if you are on your back in the snow and I'm on top I will be the one controlling the action. That way I won't hurt my leg again."

"That makes sense," the woman replied. "I'm going to freeze my ass off but here goes. " Taking her ski jacket off she put it down on the snow for a blanket, then pulled off her jeans. She took her panties off as Fitswell took off his jacket and unstrapped his walker. She helped him out of his jeans while being careful not to hurt his injured leg and pulled off his jockey shorts. Kneeling at his feet she pressed her knees firmly against the jacket as she brought her lips up to his shaft.

His penis telescoped to its full eighteen inches as she took it into her mouth. But Fitswell didn't come way out here to Idaho's cold

35

snowdrifts just to get blown. He was here for the tightest fit his penis had ever felt. *It was time to get on with business.*

As soon as he became fully erect, Fitswell roughly pushed her down onto the ski jacket. The ski jacket wasn't large enough to shield her whole body from the cold snow below her. Her upper back hit the cold snow. Worse, the ski jacket was on two feet of snow. The force of her body weight drove part of the jacket into the cold white powder which made cold wet snow push over it into direct contact with her back and half of her ass.

As he plunged deep inside her, he thought of how nice it would have been to have a large blanket. Nice for her that is. But that wasn't the point. He wanted her to freeze her ass off. As he plunged inside her he thought of her as his blanket__a human blanket. *Which is all any of them are good for anyway,* he told himself. *Human blankets to be used and discarded.*

At first she was visibly aroused, having never felt this kind of sexual excitement before. But for for Dick there was no way out. His arms sunk deep into the snow as he plunged his cock deep inside her. It was like doing pushups in the snow but at least he had a warm body beneath his torso. His penis felt warm from her hot wetness. But that only lasted so long. Had he come right away it would have been alright for both of them. But as she got colder the excitement started to ebb. Dick's arms started to feel the icy jabbing of little needles drawing his attention away from the warm sucking wetness around his penis, making it hard for him to come.

She started to shiver from the snow cradling her back, ass, neck and the back of her head, as Fitswell continued to pummel her body deep into the cold white powder. Her genitals started to convulse as they tightened, loosened, then squeezed around Dick's 18 inch member. The colder she got the more they convulsed and the tighter she got around his shaft.

He felt a vice grip clamping down on his penis. His arms continued to get colder from being buried deep in the snow keeping him from focusing upon the tightness enveloping his cock. Had he been in bed with the thermostat set at a reasonable level he would have revelled in prolonging the sexual act. Now all he could think about was getting it over with.

Suddenly the lights in the nearby condo came on just when he started coming in little spurts. As the sirens got louder, he suddenly realized--*They are coming after me.*

Squad cars started to pull up into the parking lot a hundred feet away. Dick Fitswell jumped up and hurriedly started putting his pants back on as the blonde struggled to get out of the snow. But neither of them could move fast enough. Dick was pulling one leg of his jeans up his right leg as the first police officer caught up to them as the blonde tried to find her clothes off in the snow a few feet away.

"You are both under arrest," the officer snarled.

Other officers came up, each one trying to be the first at the pair with his handcuffs. Five minutes later, they were thrusting Fitswell and the blonde into the back seat of a squad car as more lights were turned on in the condos surrounding them. Fitswell felt the cuffs tear into his wrists. The officer who had cuffed him had not been very gentle.

The blonde sat next to him in the back of the squad car staring into space all the way to the police station. "What are we being charged with?" Fitswell asked the officer.

"Indecent exposure, for one thing," the officer replied. "And I'm sure you will be charged with a couple other things. There are going to be some very pissed off people such as the DA who is going to want to throw the book at you, not to mention the judge. There were little kids watching you and your perverted girlfriend. The parents aren't too happy about it."

Fitswell continued to feel the bite of the cuffs into his wrists. Then he said under his breath--"Fuck this shit. I'm never going skiing again."

Dick Fitswell in Hong Kong

FITSWELL'S DREAM

Seen from the large windows of the Pink Giraffe nightclub twenty stories up, the view of the Hong Kong harbor is breath taking. One of the three busiest ports in the world Hong Kong is considered one of the most spectacular and romantic cities in the world. The scene of countless movies and the setting for hundreds of books Hong Kong cemented a well-deserved reputation as a bridge where the East meets the West where goods of every description can be bought--a shoppers paradise unequaled in the world. Now numbering eight million inhabitants, the city never sleeps. From the Pink Giraffe one sees hundreds of boats and ships of every size in the harbor. The Queen Mary, one of the largest and most luxurious ocean liners, is anchored less than a mile from the Pink Giraffe. Close by are Chinese junks, which at first appearance are rickety wooden cabin cruisers deserving of the name and description, junks. Hundred foot yachts of the super-rich mingle with the other boats and ships. The Pink Giraffe and much of Hong Kong's hotels and shopping are on the Kowloon side of the harbor. Dominating the harbor looms Victoria Peak, over 1600 feet straight up with its tram transporting tourists to the British style restaurant at the top. It is here that the wealthiest Chinese in the city live in their opulent mansions, their Rolls Royce's parked outside or locked away in garages. Below Victoria Peak are some of the finest hotels in the world, many built by the Brits as enduring monuments to a style that is timeless out of concrete, glass, and wood that blends the old world with the ultra-modern. Shimmering in the light with its panorama bristling with water, tall buildings and expressways, Hong Kong is unforgettable. Only one thing existed on its landscape this night of July 15th, 1999 to mar this bright jewel and that was Dick Fitswell, prowling through the Suzie Wong district (where most of the cities prostitutes live) in his never ending quest for the perfect fit.

****

"Fuck all this glamour and romance. That's only for writers like Jack Corbett who have their heads in the sand. That guy can't even get laid in a girl scout camp. I'm the guy people really want to listen to because I am getting laid all the time and all those writers, artists, film producers and other dead beats aren't. They are all pussies," said Fitswell as he watched a family of Chinese cooking their noodles in an alley.

Most of the apartments in the Suzie Wong district measure only 12 feet by 10. People are on waiting lists for months and sometimes years to get these apartments provided by the state which gives new meaning to the description poor. The laundry is hung out to dry outside the walls of most of the buildings in the area. Meals are typically eaten outside in alleys since the apartments are too small to provide the luxury of kitchen facilities. The Suzie Wong district and most of Hong Kong and Kowloon contrast sharply with the lush residential districts of the wealthy with their large homes and penthouses.

"I love it here. This place is a paradise for a guy like me. The people are so poor they will do anything for a buck and I'm just the man to take advantage of them," said Fitswell as he stamped his cigarette out in the alley. "I could probably have a man killed for fifty bucks here. Life is cheap and getting a woman's gotta be cheaper than dirt."

A scraggly Chinese woman approached him, like an old hag straight out of a Boris Korlaff film. Her skin was a mass of wrinkles, her body undernourished from years of having to do without which resulted in a face filled with so many lines that it resembled a road map of New York City. Yet........she couldn't be much over forty-five. "Poor people like her," Fitswell reflected, "usually die much earlier than practically anywhere else."

"Hey you--you American?" the woman asked Fitswell in pidgin English.

"Yes and don't try to sell me anything unless it's pussy," Fitswell replied.

"Pussy?" the woman asked. I no underestand pussy. I come ask if you like a woman."

"What kind of woman?"

"A love woman," the old hag replied. "You wanta fuckee?"

"Maybe. What are you babbling about?"

"I have beautiful daughter. You American. You much likee."

This I will have to see, Fitswell thought. *How can a woman this ugly have a beautiful daughter? But this is Hong Kong and in Hong Kong all things are possible.*

"How do I know your daughter is beautiful?"

"I have picture. See," the woman replied as she pulled out a small color Polaroid print.

The quality of the picture left something to be desired. In the middle of it was a yellow stain that probably came from someone accidentally spilling food on it. Still, it was obvious that the Chinese girl in the picture was a looker or at least had been at the time the picture was taken.

"Now that is cheap ass photography if I've ever seen any," Fitswell replied. "But your daughter looks very pretty in that picture. Good thing Jack Corbett didn't take that picture."

"My daughter, she is very pretty--yes," the woman replied happily. But dis Jack Corbett...who is he? I do not understand Inglish very good."

"Never mind him," said Fitswell. "He's an asshole. He uses digital cameras and makes women look better than they are in real life. Which makes him a liar. I would never believe a woman he takes pictures of looks the same as she appears in his pictures."

"I no understand," said the woman. "You likee my daughter?"

"Yes. I would like to meet her."

"I take you to her. She is not far."

"How much for your daughter?"

"Only five Hong Kong dollah. She very good."

Very cheap, Fitswell thought. *Well below the ten dollars I had hoped for. A bargain if she's anything like her picture.*

"Follow me," the old woman said. "Not far."

Fitswell followed the hag two blocks to a rundown apartment building following her through the entrance being careful to make sure no one was following him. He had heard of many foreigners, especially Americans, walking into such places who were never seen again. In all likelihood someone had lurked in the shadows to bludgeon them in the head or stab them to death. He followed her up a narrow flight of steps to the building's fourth floor and entered a small apartment. He couldn't believe what he saw. It was like they said--about 120 square feet. The little sitting room they entered was far smaller than even that. The whole place had been subdivided into two small rooms.

There was a couch in the sitting room. In front of it stood a small stove that was obviously used to heat the place on cold days. *Probably use dried up human feces mixed with whatever is handy for fuel,* Fitswell thought. *These dumb fuckers can't afford much of anything else.*

41

Hearing Fitswell and the old woman enter the apartment the daughter came out of the bedroom to greet them. "Mama san, you bring someone back. He very handsome," the daughter said. "I only like handsome men."

The daughter was far more than Fitswell expected. Standing over five feet eight she was much taller than the average Chinese woman in Hong Kong or the southern territories which were only a few miles away. Her waist was slender which was typical of many Chinese women but unlike most her body had the right curves. She had not bothered to cover her breasts which were full with the most succulent nipples he had seen in a long time. She wore her freshly washed thick black hair long and to her waist. Fitswell immediately fell in love with her.

"Do you want some tea?" the daughter asked.

"Please," Fitswell replied, his eyes filled with lust as he took a seat on the couch.

The young woman went over to a little pot resting on a little burner that was plugged into an electrical outlet and filled a single cup with the tea that they kept for special guests. Then she sat next to him on the couch and pressed her thigh against his.

"Give me five Hong Kong dollah now. Then we can relax," the young woman said.

Dick Fitswell reached deep into his pocket for a five Hong Kong dollar coin and handed it to the girl as the old woman went into the bedroom, after telling them--"I get room ready. Make nice and clean." As the door to the bedroom closed behind her Fitswell felt the young woman's hand resting on his lap. Fitswell started to feel a warm sensation move up his groin. The young Chinese girl opened his zipper and pulled out his schlong.

"This is living it up," said Fitswell under his breath. "I need to do a recording about all of this. Mainland China has over a billion people, most of them poor. Hong Kong has eight million. Any man who doesn't try Chinese is a damn fool. You can have your pick of this huge crop on the cheap. And here I understand women really

42

know how to treat their men. It is the Oriental way to treat men like kings and it is the woman's job to serve them. And I have heard that oriental women are tighter than Americans . And that's what I am here for. The perfect fit "

The old hag came out of the bedroom, her face beaming. "The bedroom is ready. Just for you. Finish tea so I can make this room clean."

Dick Fitswell greedily finished his cup of tea, eager to try out the freshly cleaned bedroom. The young Chinese woman led him gently by his hand into the bedroom. Once again, he could barely believe what he saw. The bed took up the whole room, which considering that both rooms totaled only 120 square feet should not have been surprising. The Chinese girl did not waste time, pulling off her clothes; then she finished the job of unzipping his zipper and pulling off his pants and jockey shorts.

She grabbed his penis as she edged onto the bed, lay down on her back and roughly pulled him on top of her by his penis. His schlong, normally 18 inches long rapidly expanded to 19 inches, the longest that it had ever been. Outside the bedroom in the sitting room Dick Fitswell heard a noise that sounded like a vacuum cleaner. *Probably the old woman vacuuming the place*, he said to himself.

Still grasping his schlong the Chinese girl spread her legs and started to insert it into her opening. But Fitswell would have none of it. She was too good to waste. He knew he would want her the next night and the night after as soon as he entered her. Thinking *she's awfully tight* he said out loud............"You make me bigger than any girl has ever managed before. "

Pulling his penis out of her, Fitswell got up out of bed, picked her up and set her down again so that her body rested on her stomach. *I have to do this one right*, he thought. *She' s not excited enough. I don't normally pay for this even though it's costing me next to nothing. I want her to be mine. I want her to want me more than she's wanted any man before so I can keep coming back here.* Getting into bed behind her he started licking her privates, probing with his tongue, at first just part way into her opening, before sticking it in as far as it would go. The girl started to get wet but Fitswell kept his tongue deep inside her until he could taste her wetness flow copiously throughout his mouth and all over his face. The woman started to arch her body upwards as she thrust her buttocks firmly into his face.

She wants me. They all do, Dick Fitswell said to himself. *Now I will make her mine.*

He turned her over as she spread her legs and jammed his 19 inch schlong deep inside her. In spite of her wetness she felt tight. In the background he could still hear the vacuum cleaner. *Has to be one of those little mini vacuums many Chinese have,* he thought. *It is just like those little stereo systems they sell all over the Orient. In places like Tokyo, Singapore, Bangkok, Shanghai and here in Hong Kong. Unless someone's filthy rich space is too expensive. Rents are outrageous and people won't tolerate the high noise levels of high powered stereo systems. People live close together in small apartments and houses right up next to each other. There's little room for big stereo systems. Probably the same way with vacuum cleaners. You really don't need a large vacuum cleaner to clean a small place and there's little space to store it.*

The young Chinese woman started to wrap her legs around his waist squeezing him in with her well muscled thighs. This drew him even deeper inside of her. He could feel it now........the sensation from almost every inch of his penis being sucked deep inside her. Then.......just as he really started to get into it, just as he started to focus on the exquisite fit, the length of her full body tightly against him, her tight nipples jammed firmly into his chest, an overwhelming drowsiness started to overcome him.

Home at last. Deep inside a woman with a nearly perfect figure Dick Fitswell drifted off. Outside the bedroom the droning of the vacuum cleaner took over what remained of his consciousness. Although the sensation of the tight pussy around his cock continued he closed his eyes and started to fall asleep. No longer looking at the woman he was inside, and unable to see her

44

through closed eyelids he dreamed about a vacuum cleaner nozzle as he listened on. His nineteen inch penis was thrust deep up the vacuum cleaner's nozzle as he heard the machine's little motor suck the come right out of him.

Dick Fitswell was asleep. The young Chinese woman gently lifted him off her body as the old mama san came into the room. The two women rifled Dick Fitswell's pockets where they found a thousand American dollars. The tea had done its job.

Dick Fitswell goes to Canada

"But Doc, I'm Dick Fitswell, the man after the perfect fit. You are asking too much out of me."

"Dick.....You are thirty-five now and no longer in your prime. It might mean more than life and death. It just could be your sanity."

"So when can I return to some serious fucking?"

"That's up to you but I suggest you take at least a month off."

******

A long past his prime, Dick Fitswell while giving a speech at the Pattaya, Thailand Expatriate's club on how to stay on top of Thai women.

"Those damn bitches have been doing this to me. They just don't understand that I've been trying to do them a favor. I give them my best shots, right up their pussies of the best elixir in the world, and what do they do to show their appreciation? They act like bitches. Caused my blood pressure to get out of line and now that Doctor says he can't just give me an antibiotic----he tells me I've gotta take it easy and quit fucking them for awhile. But I can't. So I'm going somewhere where I'm not going to be tempted. Where there's either no women or where the women are too damn ugly. I'm heading to Canada."

Wending its way through the Yukon wilds, the Canadian Pacific passenger train was now carrying the most precious cargo it had been entrusted to in years–the live carcass of Dick Fitswell complete with its eighteen inch pleasure rod. But Dick wasn't too happy with his situation. He thought about what he would do during the long nights ahead of him as the train approached Dawson, his final destination. Almost worse than ordering him to give up women, the Doc had asked him to stay away from alcohol. The train got into the station at 2 AM. Dick got himself a room at a near by hotel and passed out almost immediately after hitting the pillow. It had been a long train ride with no booze and not a single good looking women aboard.

Dick spent the next afternoon exploring the town, but the sun went down early, so he found a restaurant and had a reindeer steak, a local favorite. He hated doing it but went back to the hotel where he settled down with a book, *The Seduction of the Perfect Woman*, when the lights suddenly went out.

"Shit. Damn electricity's gone out. That's what I get for going to a Socialist Country. Now what am I going to do?"

The thought of a bar intrigued him even though he had promised himself not to drink. *A bar in Dawson's gotta have lights. Electricity probably goes out here pretty often and these Canadians probably cannot stand being around each other for very long without getting shitfaced. That's what I've seen in those old Dawson Dog sled movies while the men were looking for gold in the Klondike. They will have kerosene lamps or a generator or something.* Although it had gotten dark Dick Fitswell could still find his way around since the Yukon sky never got inky black this time of the year. He had walked only several blocks from his hotel when he saw it--The Hunter Bar. *Alright,* he nearly said aloud, *It's got the right kind of name. And it looks disreputable enough. I think I'll go in and cause some shit.*

Inside he found total chaos and immediately fell in love with the place. There were few whites in the bar but plenty of Eskimos and Indians. Dick Fitswell had heard that the Canadians had felt so badly about what they did to the Eskimos and Indians in the Yukon that the government put them all on welfare as long as they hung out in the towns and couldn't make a living hunting and fishing. Each dispossessed Indian or Eskimo got $3000 Canadian dollars per month as long as he or she met the government's requirements. Which was basically to get drunk and stay drunk.

Dick found the prettiest woman in the bar sitting on a barstool and sat up next to her ordering a lemonade from the bartender. He couldn't tell whether she was an Eskimo or Indian and didn't care since he was planning to get her drunk on her butt which shouldn't cost much since she was already half way there. He was about to make his move when he heard a loud thud, turned around, and saw that an Eskimo male who had been sleeping it off on one of the tables had just rolled off and fallen to the floor. The man was so drunk that the fall hadn't awakened him so everyone in the place decided to just let him continue sleeping it off on the floor.

"They ought to rename this place Comatoseville," Fitswell said to the woman sitting next to him.

"What did you say? I do not understand you. But do you have a cigarette?"

"Sure...and let me light one for you," Dick said to the woman as he reached for one of his Marlboros, put it in his mouth, lit it, then handed it to her. "Can I get you anything? Beer? Whiskey? How about a Tequila? That's what real women drink back where I"m from?"

"Get me some Vodka. That is what Eskimo women drink. I'm Eskimo. Did you know that?"

"I've never met anyone who's Eskimo," Dick replied. Then he ordered her vodka from the bartender.

She was getting to be pretty drunk after the first one. By the time he ordered her fourth vodka, the woman was almost falling off her barstool. Suddenly another woman was in their faces shouting to his newfound Eskimo, "You give him to me. He is too good for you." But although she was drunk Fitswell's companion somehow mustered up enough presence of mind to deal with the intruder. The Hunter Bar was not the cleanest place in the world and the bartender who had spent most of his life on welfare wasn't good about picking up the beer bottles and glasses the previous

48

customers had left there. The Eskimo woman grabbed a beer bottle lying in front of her and smashed the other woman in the head with it. The intruder dropped to the floor, blood pouring out of her head. Everyone in the place let her lie there, bleeding.

"Now I feel like a woman should," the Eskimo said. "I love blood. It makes me want to have sex."

"I'm in trouble now," Dick Fitswell told himself. "The Doc told me to stay away from women and not to have sex for at least a month."

"Do you want to suck my tits?" the woman asked him as she took off the fur t shirt she was wearing.

Fitswell looked at them and observed that they were far better than he expected in a place like this. The woman had medium size breasts with very large and very firm nipples that appeared to be bursting with milk. But before he could even bend down to take one of them into his mouth, the woman was on his lap, thrusting a tit in his face. Gratefully he wrapped his mouth around a tit and started sucking it. It started to ooze wetness into his mouth, then it started to harden as it spurted liquid down his throat.

But it didn't taste like milk. "Nirvana," Fitswell shouted. "Booze. This tit's filled with alcohol" as he pulled away for a second or two, then crunched down on it again, and continued to suck------ this time deliriously, like a drug addict breathing in from his crack pipe. Somehow the tits being full of alcohol didn't surprise him since everyone in the bar seemed to practically live there and the Eskimo had probably long ago become one with her alcohol.

Suddenly the woman pulled her tit out of his mouth and said to him: "You will get no more until you fuck me. But you have to go home with me."

"You lead and I'll follow", Fitswell told her.

They walked almost a half mile before they found her place just on the outskirts of town. The last few hundred yards they had to walk through a foot and a half blanket of snow. Fitswell was thankful for wearing boots. Then he saw it----the place where she lived--and blinked his eyes in disbelief. "A fucking igloo. You live in a real igloo? I've never been in one of those before."

She knelt down on the snow in front of him and started to crawl through the short, narrow entryway that led to the warmth inside. Still a little light headed from sucking her tit, Fitswell watched her tight ass wiggle as she worked her way into the igloo's interior. He followed closel behind her, saying to himself, "I don't want to lose sight of that ass."

When they got inside she lit an oil lamp, then lay back on a fur that covered one end of the igloo and motioned for him to join her. She pulled off her jeans, then she pulled off the fur panties she wore to keep her privates warm. "What a body!" Fitswell exclaimed aloud. "I've watched too many movies that showed all you Eskimo women as being fat."

"Oh no. Many of us are not fat. I've seen those movies too. The thing is most of us like to fuck and that helps us stay thin. The trouble with most white women is they don't want to fuck enough because they'd rather be fat."

I want to fuck her so bad, Fitswell said to himself. *But my doctor told me not to. I will have to just satisfy myself with sucking her tits.* And then he fell upon her and started sucking the other breast, the one he had neglected back in the bar. As the alcohol started to hit him he started to feel at peace with himself----a peace he had not felt since his last drink.

The next ten minutes he spent going from one breast to the other...sucking them dry as the Eskimo became increasingly excited. Her legs threshed wildly about as she jammed her bosom into his face, before she finally reached down and felt Fitswell's penis which had swollen up to its full eighteen inches. "Fuck me," she cried out. "Fuck me now. So we can do it again and again."

Shit...what am I going to do now? Fitswell asked himself then said to her----"I can't. I can't fuck you. Doctor's orders. But I want to."

50

"What?" the woman screamed. "What do you mean you can't. Fuck me. Fuck me. I want you in me now."

"I'm sorry, but I can't. I have high blood pressure and the doctor told me not to fuck anyone for at least a month. But I will be happy to keep sucking your tits."

"You fucker. You are not going to fuck me?"

"No. I can't. I want to but I can't."

"Fuck you." Then the woman turned around and screamed, "Polarina, take him. He's yours."

******

There is a lot of truth to the Bigfoot or Sasquatch legends . Hundreds of years ago there was a band of Eskimo living near what is now Dawson who believed that the highest form of bravery was exhibited by the hunter who could mate with a Polar Bear and live. This band of hunters including its women and children kept to itself and zealously guarded its darkest secrets from other Eskimo bands. Very few men tried it and most of them who did, were killed. The race that sprung from these illicit matings had been believed to have died out but every now and then a sighting was reported.

Fitswell never saw the shrouded figure crouching in the dark recesses of the igloo. Aroused by the screams of the Eskimo woman, the beast sprung onto the fur blanket Fitswell and the woman were lying on. Then it jumped on top of Fitswell. It took just two seconds for Fitswell to suddenly realize that he had no chance. Until that moment Polarina had been releasing her pent up sexual desires by masturbating.

Fitswell felt paw like hands rip his pants off then he felt furry fingers grasp his eighteen inch member. Already stiff and erect it all happened so fast that he didn't lose his erection as Polarina knelt over him and thrust his penis into her vagina. Although he was horrified by the sight of the gigantic humanoid hovering over him Fitswell's penis had a mind of its own and in familiar territory went into autopilot mode as Polarina started to thrust against him. Even worse..........it was a tight fit. It was a great fit. The best he had ever experienced. Frightened by the apparition astride him but with his penis engorged in a throbbing tightness that kept sucking it in, swallowing it, relaxing, then tightening up again Fitswell pushed his body tightly up into Polarina. Two minutes later, Fitswell started to spurt uncontrollable bursts of jetting semen.

The trouble was, Polarina, as sex starved as she was, didn't stop. Lying down across Fitswell Polarina reached underneath him and pulled him tight against her furry body. She didn't climb off of him for two hours. By this time the Eskimo woman sobered up enough to realize what she had done and called in the Eskimo version of the ambulance------the dog sled. Fitswell was driven to the hospital where he was immediately put into Dawson's version of Intensive Care.

Dick Fitswell meets the socialized Canadian Health Care System

"I gotta get out of this place," Dick Fitswell yelled at the Canadian doctor walking down the hallway outside his room. Since he had gotten there Dick Fitswell had noticed that the Canadian doctors were easy to spot in their Royal Canadian Mounted Police uniforms. The doctors being impoverished since the socialized health care system had taken over the country had been only too glad when surplus uniforms became available to them now that the Canadian Mounties had been forced to wear more modest clothing such as suits and ties. The nurses, who were even more impoverished than the doctors, wore practically nothing.

"I need a fucking nurse," Fitswell screamed, hoping someone would hear him. "My dick is hurting." But no one came. The persistent throbbing in his scrotum had gotten worse. Fitswell looked around the room nervously for a button he could push to ring a nurse. Instead he saw a strip of cloth that had been glued to the little dresser next to his bed. On it someone had scrawled with a magic marker-------"Your nurse is Eskola. To be serviced please ring the bell on top of the dresser." And there it was. A bell for ringing the nurse. But it was one of those cow bells one used to find in old barnyards.

Unfucking unbelievable, Fitswell muttered to himself, as he rang the bell. Within five minutes his nurse appeared. It was the Eskimo woman he had followed back to her igloo. The same one who had sicced Polarina upon him--the same one who was responsible for the sickening pain he was now feeling in his testicles.

The woman recognized him immediately and started to grin. He had not noticed it in the darkness of the bar or the gloomy recesses of her igloo but she was missing some of her front teeth

53

which made her look like an overgrown wood chuck when she smiled. Then he noticed that she was still wearing the same fur hat she was wearing when he first met her in the bar.

Oh shit, he whispered to himself. *Now I've really got to get back to the United States.*

"Whatever you are thinking, stop thinking it," said the nurse, as if she could read his thoughts. "You are mine. As long as you are here. If you ever get out of here that is."

"I want a doctor," Fitswell replied. "I have a right to see a doctor."

"Very well. I'll get you one right away," the nurse replied as she hurried out of the room. But not for long. Within two minutes she came back followed by a thick set middle aged man wearing a Canadian Mountie uniform.

"Dick Fitswell," I want you to meet your doctor, Doctor Plummer. He specializes in Penises and is very interested in yours."

"Why is he so interested in me?" Dick asked.

"You've made quite a reputation for yourself my boy. Not only in the United States but even up here in Canada. You are the one and only Dick Fitswell, aren't you? The man with the eighteen inch schlong who's on a quest for the perfect fit."

"Yes. I have to admit," Dick replied. "I am God's gift to women."

"Correction," the Doc replied. "Was."

"What do you mean was?" Dick asked anxiously.

"What the Doctor means," said Eskola, "is that since you were raped by Polarina you have suffered some severe injuries. Your once eighteen inch penis is now only nine and a half inches long. But it gets worse. You have been severely bruised and the doctor thinks the bruising's permanent. Your sex drive's never going to be the same again."

"Bullshit," Fitswell screamed at them. "I am Dick Fitswell and my life's ambition is to find the perfect fit. Nothing's going to stop me."

"That's the whole point," the doctor replied, raising his voice for the first time. "You will be stopped. I have discussed the whole situation with the other doctors in this hospital and they've taken the matter up with the state department. The word's come down from the Prime Minister himself."

"What do you mean, the word's come down from the Prime Minister himself?" Fitswell shot back. I want safe asylum to the American embassy."

"Too late for that, Dick," said the Doc. "You have been declared a national health care risk. We will have to operate."

"Operation! I don't need an operation. I need to get out of this Canadian hell hole."

"You can yell and scream all you want. No you can't," the doc contradicted himself. "Nurse...give him a taste of the taser."

Eskola pulled the battery operated taser gun out of the little holster she was wearing on her belt, jerked open Fitswell's hospital gown, and thrust its tip against his upper thigh as she squeezed the trigger. Fitswell felt the shock immediately as his body recoiled. But Eskola held the tip relentlessly against his thigh while glaring down at him maliciously. She pulled away from him at the last moment just as she sensed he was about to pass out. Fitswell lay there shaking, unable to move. Gradually his mind started to focus. What it focused upon was the Doctor's face leaning close to his. He saw the doctor's mouth move. Then he heard the words.

"The average Canadian male has a penis that's five inches long. The Prime Minister has ruled that yours constitutes a national security risk since if you become even more well known here, all our women will want you. A lot of them will fuck you and you will no doubt get some of them pregnant. The effect of your genes being carried by Canadian children is unknown. His advisers think that the long term effect will be to increase the size of Canadian men's penises and the long term consequences of that are unknown. Therefore it's something to avoid. So tonight I am going to operate on you. You will end up having a dick that is exactly five inches long."

"I will kill you then," Dick Fitswell yelled at the doctor. "I will hunt you down. You can never hide from the Fitz Express."

"The hell I can't. First, you will be deported back to the United States. But before I'm done with you I'm going to burn a little brand into your forehead which will read LP. Stands for Little Penis. If you ever try to get back into our country they will see this brand on your forehead and not allow you across the border, and if you get across the border, everyone will be alerted. You will be found, caught, and executed."

Then the doctor stomped out of the room followed by his nurse, who kept looking back at Fitswell with a knowing smile. Shaken by the news and feeling weakened by the electricity that had recently surged throughout his body, Fitswell passed out. Then.....he started to feel someone warm lying up against him.

"How long have I been asleep?" Fitswell asked.

"Only a half hour," Eskola replied.

"What are you doing here?"

"I'm here because I want you to fuck me."

"Fuck you? Why?"

"Because you still have nine and a half inches. I've never gotten nine and a half inches rammed up me before."

The half hour's sleep had eaten away at the rage Dick had been feeling. Eskola's warm body lying up against him had already gotten him partially erect. Suddenly the thought of having his penis reduced to only 5 inches seemed far off in the future.

Putting his hands between Eskola's legs he pried her knees apart as she pulled on his penis. Within seconds he was inside her as she thrashed around on the bed.

"Stick it in deeper," she yelled out at him. I want every inch. Five inches were never enough. That's why it has always been my dream to leave Canada."

Egged on by the excited Eskimo now attached to him by his long shaft Dick crushed his body deeper into hers, somehow finding an extra inch or two. And for his efforts was rewarded with her screaming: "I feel impaled. Dick, dismember me with that penis of yours. Spread me wide."

And so it went. He pulsed and she throbbed. He got light headed and she fell instantly in love. And finally the inevitable occurred. The sperm bank erupted as he came jetting what seemed to be endless spurts of the finest juices that she had ever felt bursting in her box. When it was over, Eskola put her cheek up next to his and started to cry. Fitswell let her tears run down his chin as he started to contemplate what life would be like wearing only a five inch dick. Then she left him as she went on her rounds to see her other patients. An hour later she came back but this time she brought the doctor with her.

"Okay Dick. Your time has come. Now we are going to make you into Dickie," the doctor said coldly. Then turning to Eskola said----"Okay babe. Secure him so he can't move."

There was a button on the side of the hospital bed that Fitswell had never seen before. Eskola bent over him, and pushed it in. Suddenly he felt his arms and legs being seized. Steel spring like arms sprung from the bed, grasped his legs and tightened, spreading his legs wide. At the same time another pair of mechanical arms found his wrists, clamped hard onto them, then pulled his arms down across the bed so that he resembled a man being crucified in the horizontal position.

"Okay, Eskola. We got him where we want him. Now pull his pants off and hold his balls while I inject them full of pain killer."

"What! You aren't going to put me asleep first?" Dick yelled. "Why you fat little prick," he told the Doc as Eskola removed his pants leaving his privates in full view.

And then Dick Fitswell saw truth for the first time in his life as Eskola kneeled over him with the syringes. Truth was the sharp edged knives and other surgical instruments the Doctor started laying on his chest. No way out. He would have to watch the whole procedure. His own blood spilling out of his penis and sack. With the amputation of his beloved stalk. The removal of the head of his penis, then watching the Doc sew it back onto his shortened shaft. It was the horror of all horrors to have to watch his own dismemberment. Even worse....he could never be Dick Fitswell again.

Dick Fitswell and the surgeon's knife

"This is the end of the world," Dick Fitswell screamed to himself. "My cock. My gift to womankind will be lost. And with it all hope for humanity. And it's going to hurt like a motherfucker even if the Doc shoots my balls and shaft full of Novocain feel alike."

The Doc felt the surgeon's knife in his hand as he checked its balance. Then narrowed his eyes as he noticed that something wasn't right. "Too dull," he remarked to Eskola, the Eskimo nurse now standing next to him. "Get me another one." Eskola went a few feet over to a small chest of drawers where the Doc kept most of his instruments, shuffled around through the drawers then called out to him: "There isn't a single surgeon's knife left here."

"Damn the luck, "the Doc muttered. I used the last one to shave with. These damn Canadian razors aren't worth much these days. Even Fitswell doesn't deserve a dull blade. But I guess we will have to use it anyway."

"Not to worry," I've got my hunting knife with me," Eskola replied as she felt for it resting in the scabbard around her waist. "We Eskimos use these things for everything and they have to be sharp."

"Hold onto it," as I shoot his testicles up with the syringe.

Dick Fitswell's testicles and cock stood exposed to the world as he lay there firmly clasped by the hospital bed's mechanical arms with the Doc moving in on him, the syringe firmly in his grip. Gently the Doc fondled Dick's balls as he prepared to pierce them with the needle.

"This is going to hurt like hell Dick. But after I get your balls all shot up, we'll give you a few minutes before I inject your shaft. That won't hurt nearly as much."

Suddenly Dick felt an idea hit him like a jolt of lightning opening his eyes. A warm feeling came over his body as his confidence returned. "Eskola", he called out. "Let's blow this pop stand and go fuck in your igloo. Remember my coming in you just a couple hours ago. Imagine me doing that to you all night long?"

Eskola nearly dropped the knife. It was the words she had been longing to hear for a long time. Someone actually wanted to fuck her. And not just anyone. This wasn't just anyone. This was Dick Fitswell, the American who got all the women. "He really wants to fuck me," she whispered to herself. "He already has but he's just said he wants to fuck me all night long. I must be good."

"Do you promise, Dick? Promise to fuck me all night long?"

"I promise, Eskola. When I fucked you this afternoon I suddenly realized how much you mean to me."

"How about tomorrow and how about the next day?" Eskola pleaded.

"I will fuck you all week long, Eskola," Dick Fitswell lied. "I knew in my heart that someday I'd meet someone just like you and now you have become a dream come true."

"What's going on?" screamed the Doc. Give me that knife, Eskola. To hell with the anesthetic. We've got work to do."

"Fuck you Doc. What have you ever done for me?"

"If you value your job, you will give me that knife," yelled the Doctor.

"What's a job anyway compare to a good fuck? Dick's given me a better offer, Doc. Sorry."

The knife that she used to skin Caribou, kill grizzly bears, and cut blubber into thin strips was a very large knife with a twelve inch blade. It's handle was large and heavy which furnished a solid grip. The knife was as heavy as many pistols. She had bought it from a bunch of Mexicans who had gotten lost in Igloo land. Like many Mexican hunting knives it had a handle guard that resembled brass knuckles. Which such knives were often employed as giving its owner the option of stabbing his adversary to death, cutting off his head with a single slashing blow, or bashing out his teeth with its handle guard. Tired of talking and tired of screaming, Eskola turned on the Doctor then she swung the handle end of the knife at his skull. There was a sickening thud as the knife's handle guard connected with his head. The Doc slumped to the floor.

Eskola then found the button on Dick Fitswell's hospital bed and pushed it which released the mechanical arms that had been pinioning his arms and legs. As the steel arms protracted back into the bed Dick Fitswell jumped up, a free man at last. Then....calmly, the pair left the hospital to Eskola's dog sled and huskies that she had parked outside.

The cold Canadian air was bracing and Dick Fitswell wasn't ready for it since he was still wearing his hospital gown. But there had been no time to lose. It took only fifteen minutes for the dogs to pull them to Eskola's igloo. By this time Dick felt he would lose the penis that had just narrowly escaped the surgeon's knife to frostbite. But inside the igloo was warm.

He almost tripped over Polarina who was lounging lazily next to the fire in the center of the igloo. The humanoid that was half polar bear and half eskimo lay on its side with its eyes half closed. A half empty bottle of whiskey lay by her side. "I owe you one big time," Dick Fitswell whispered to himself as he stared nervously at the huge monstrosity.

"You must be hungry," Eskola said to him. "I will feed you in an hour but first I want you to fuck me." Then she pointed out a huge polar bear rug a few feet from the fire. "Take off your clothes," she ordered.

"I didn't see that Polar Bear rug here the last time I was here. Where'd you get it."

"Oh that. Polarina killed the bear for me yesterday. Then skinned it for me as a present. Killed it with her bare claws."

"You mean bear claws," Fitswell added.

"Yes. Bear claws. Since birth Polarina has been slightly afflicted."

Relieved that he still had nine and a half inches of his original eighteen inch cock, Dick Fitswell gratefully took off his hospital gown and lay across the rug as Eskola went down on him. He became aroused as soon as her lips brushed against his dick. *Must be because of all the excitement*, he remarked to himself. Then he started to study the face that was busily milking his member. *Not that bad*, he remarked to himself. *I don't know why I didn't fuck her in the first place.* Then he remembered his American doctor's orders to stay away from women for a couple months. *Bad medical advice though. Dick Fitswell's penis must be served. Like a fine Ferrari it should be driven hard and not kept in the garage. That doctor never knew what he was talking about. And to think of all the girls I could have serviced in all that time that I've lost.*

Eskola sensed that he was close to coming, then spit his dick from her mouth while Dick mind churned. *I'll make her do all the work. I have something important to do tonight. Let her wear herself out.* Then he let her mount him. He didn't come for fifteen minutes. After he finished squirting his precious elixir into her, she collapsed on his chest. It had been a hard day for her at work.

Fifteen minutes later she came to and remounted him. This time it took him a half hour to come and once again she collapsed with her head on his chest. Dick Fitswell reached around her, pulled her off, and snuggled her body next to his, hoping she'd stay asleep this time.

An hour later Eskola was still sleeping next to him. Dick Fitswell started to stare intensely at Polarina who was still in a deep drunken slumber next to the fire. *No one. Nothing rapes Dick Fitswell and gets away with it,* he told himself. *If anyone's going to do any raping it's gonna be me.*

When Eskola had taken off her clothes she had left the hunting knife in its scabbard next to her. Dick Fitswell pulled the knife from the scabbard, then got up slowly and as quietly as he could to avoid waking up Eskola. "So far so good," he whispered to himself as he slowly crawled across the igloo to the sleeping humanoid by the fire.

I think I'm Ulysses, Dick Fitswell said to himself as he raised the knife above Polarina's head. *Only this isn't going to be any Cyclops,* he remarked as he drove its blade into one of Polarina's eyelids. Thrusting down onto the knife he could feel its blade cut through Polarina's eye, through her skull and into the humanoid's brain. Death was instantaneous although there was a great deal of blood spurting from out of Polarina's eye socket.

Now comes the hard part, Dick Fitswell thought as he grabbed Polarina by the arms and started dragging her to the far end of the igloo, into those same shadows where Polarina had raped him. Luckily Eskola slept on--dead to the world. Dick went back to the fire and cleaned up the blood that had spurted from Polarina.

I was sure noisy dragging Polarina out of sight, Dick Fitswell gloated to himself. *Now that would have woken anybody up. But I fucked Eskola twice and this just goes to show that I, Dick Fitswell, am the world's best fuck. I am just too much for any woman alive.*

Dick Fitswell's Religious Conversion

"I'm back. I've grown a half inch. My penis is now ten inches long," Dick Fitswell crowed,. "So I think I'll stay awhile."

Since moving into the igloo with Eskola, Dick Fitswell's penis had gotten a half inch longer. Dick attributed its new lease on life to a steady diet of fucking her four times a day. He had only been there for three days. Fucking her twice that afternoon Dick excused himself in the middle of dinner with that excuse that never seemed to fail him in the past......"Honey. I've got diarrhea. I'll be right back." Perched on the toilet seat like an ostrich in heat Dick reached into his boot for the measuring tape he always carried with him. Then he lay back and started thinking about some of the women he had reamed during the past year. Eskola's image never came up as he started to get hard. Then, satisfied with his erection Dick pulled the tape out, laying one end along the tip of his penis as he pulled the tape out to the base of his scrotum.

"Ten and an eight inches long," he gloated. "In a few days I'll be normal again. I think I'll fuck her again tonight."

Which he did but Dick Fitwell never regained his full length in that igloo. Polarina's dead body started to stink and the next night Eskola remarked as they sat around the fire together, "What's that smell?" To which Dick answered, "It's nothing babe. That used to be a song is all." But he knew that Polarina would soon start to reek and that Eskola would find her–possibly as early as the next day.

That night Dick Fitswell waited until Eskola fell sound asleep, then sneaked out of the igloo and started to hike into Dawson. As soon as he got into town he saw the train that would leave at six AM. It was now 2 AM which meant the train would remain there another four hours. Dick was amazed at this incredible display of inefficiency, then suddenly remembered that this was Canada and that in this little country efficiency was exactly a national obsession.

Wanting to be alone with his thoughts Dick Fitswell found a vacant car. There was no one in it. For half an hour he rested, then woke up to a deep resonant voice. Crying out his name, the voice called out to him: "Dick Fitswell. You have been very selfish."

Dick Fitswell looked around the railroad car for a man or something inhuman the voice could be coming from. There was no one----nothing in the car with him. Just lots of empty seats. Then he heard it again: "Dick Fitswell. I am with you always. Do not look for my source for I am the light." Dick Fitswell found the goat skin of whiskey tied to his belt, pulled out its little plastic cork, then squeezed whiskey onto his palms, which he then splashed over his face hoping it would sting enough to make the voice go away. Then he heard it again.

"Give it up Dick. There is no one in this car but us. Now listen up."

"Are you God? Dick asked. "Because if you are, I'm one up on you."

"How do you figure that?" the voice asked.

"Because I get more pussy than you."

"That's my whole point about your being selfish."

"Huh. I'm being selfish? I'm selfish? I've spread the joy of Fitswell wherever I've fucked. You call that selfish?"

"Dick. You are just a piker. You need to spread yourself around more. Haven't you noticed something strange about your dick?"

"Yeah. It's still too small."

"Dick," the voice continued. "Your dick has just grown from being nine and a half inches long to ten and a half in less than two days. That was a sign from me but you just didn't catch on did you?"

"Catch on to what?"

"That your health and the length of your penis would depend upon how much you fucked and how many women you scored with."

"Give me a break. My penis is getting bigger because I am Dick Fitswell and no one gets the better of the ole Fitz, the world's most perfect fuck."

"Dick. You are the world's best fuck but only because I have given you the power and the penis."

"Alright. Give me another sign because I don't fucking believe you."

"Dick. Look down upon thy penis."

Suddenly Dick Fitswell felt the most excruciating pain he had ever felt in his life. Polarina's raping him and nearly tearing his dick off was nothing compared to what he felt now. Blood started bursting open the capillaries in his penis. He felt unbelievable pressure in his shaft as he watched his penis shrink. What was left was a two inch shard of skin and cartilage. He almost fainted from the surge of blood that had been meant for an eighteen inch penis but which was now suddenly confined to a 2 inch underdeveloped shred of flesh. "

"Make it stop. I'll do anything you want."

"Okay. I'll give it back to you then but only for as long as you carry me with you."

His relief was instantaneous as he watched his penis grow back to its original size and the blood flow was no longer confined to its former surroundings. But it didn't stop at ten and a half inches. Dick watched it grow to first twelve inches which was the longest it had been since he had sex with Polarina, to a full fourteen inches. He felt better than ever."

"Okay Ultra Being or whatever you want to be. From now on it's just you and me," said Dick Fitswell meaning every word of it. But can you first give me back all of my original eighteen inches."

"The deed is done.

Fitswell felt a pulling pulsating sensation between his legs. When he looked down he saw that he once again had his full eighteen inches. "Nice job," he exclaimed. "You have sure made a believer out of me. What do you want me to call you?"

"Just call me Harry. Easier to remember that way."

"Alright-------what do you want me to do."

"Dick. I want you to spread yourself around more. Consider me the Father and you as my Son. You need to get around to more women. And you need to make yourself more famous."

"So who's to be the Holy Ghost or Holy Spirit?"

"Your semen. Every time you blow your wad in a woman you will be injecting her with the Holy Spirit."

"You gotta be shitting me." Then thinking back on the pain he had just felt as he watched his penis being shrunk to two inches Dick exclaimed: "I take it back. But please explain yourself."

"Dick. You need to be more of a fantasy. You know you have achieved our destiny together when you have practically every woman in the world pining away for you in their dreams. You also need to impregnate more women. To put little Fitswell's onto this earth."

"How will I know what to do? The task seems overwhelming."

"Let me guide you. Follow me and I will lead you to the light. I will visit you from time to time."

"When?"

"I have to get going."

"Don't go just yet."

"I have to. Get out of Canada, Dick."

Suddenly the car seemed empty. Dick started to look around him but the car seemed more deserted than before. An eerie silence filled the air. Whatever had been there was gone. For the first time in his life Dick felt alone.

Dick Fitswell Goes to Church

FITSWELL DISCOVERS VIAGRA
& CHEST HAIR ENHANCER!

"This is it. A perfect place for me, the world's perfect fuck," Dick Fitswell nearly shouted aloud. Been here for one month now and who would believe it, that I'd finally find myself here in church."
In the front row sat the ministers wife, a long legged blonde the shy side of thirty. *Do credit to any strip bar,* Fitswell thought to himself. *I'll bet she's one tight babe. I swear to God I'll make her squirm before I leave these Protestants.* Since his first meeting with "God" Dick Fitswell was very thorough in choosing just the right Church for a man of his position. For the past five years he had been a marketing executive for America Online, which many of his colleagues in the computer profession had denigrated by calling it "Assholes Online, Always Offline", and other descriptive epithets so he always tried harder than his counterparts by being more thorough and careful in his chosen career to make up for the low esteem which he had to suffer by working for AOL in the first place. He had analyzed over twenty-five congregations by going to a different church twice each Sunday. Whether the Church was Methodist, Episcopalian, Lutheran, or the Church of England for that matter had little part of his analysis. What counted was which denomination had the most babes of all ages, excepting the elderly. He had finally settled on a lively Church which called itself, "Brotherly and Sisterly Love for Everyone". He had never heard of it before but its Congregation numbered over three thousand and it had two services each Sunday not counting Wednesday and Thursday evening services for the night owls.

The minister and his wife impressed him the first time he saw them. *Good looking couple,* Dick thought, *but the minister's obviously a pussy. Or he wouldn't be a minister in the first place.*

69

I gotta help this woman who got stuck with him by showing her what a real man's all about." He marveled at her long trim legs and tight little ass remarking to himself—*"She's a goddess if I ever saw one. Venus on earth. Bet I can become a God with her.*

"I"ll bang her or my name's not Dick Fitswell," he vowed.

The second thing that impressed him the most was the large percentage of High School aged kids. Hundreds of them and they usually sat a few pews back. It had taken him twelve weeks to find the right church. He promised himself that he would become a church leader in less than six weeks, feeling he had no time to lose. Four weeks had passed and he felt he had made little headway in his mission. Then he saw his chance. They were counting the offering money.

Like most churches, the Church of "Brotherly and Sisterly Love for Everyone" always had at least two members from the board of Trustees count the money. It was too much of a job for one person given the congregation's size and having at least two counting the offerings minimized the risk for embezzlement. He had noticed that a man and a woman were responsible for counting the congregation's money in one of the back rooms but the man had a known drinking problem. The woman was in her early thirties, was twenty pounds overweight and Dick had decided but barely. He had started talking to her the second Sunday he had come to Church, being careful to arrive half an hour before the service started. The man who normally counted the money with her wasn't in sight. *Probably too hung over to show up, Dick Fitswell remarked to himself, which opens her up to the great Fitz persuader, my eighteen inch prod.*

Observing at the end of the service how the woman's eyes were searching the congregation for her companion, Dick ran up to her, trying to show just the right amount of compassion in his eyes. He had practiced before the mirror in his bathroom until he had mastered the technique of causing his eyes to water just the right amount. *Moist eyes appeal to a lot of women, he had decided since it makes them feel that I am a caring kind of man.*

"Gloria. Need some help counting the church's money? Seems you are short handed."

"Jim's not here. Yes. It takes us half an hour to count and to record the money. By myself it takes twice as long. Thank you." Although Dick wasn't a trustee and therefore shouldn't be counting the churches money, she respected him because he worked for AOL which she knew all about since she used AOL to get online whenever it let her connect.   "Why try anything else?" she had told her closest friends who were now in rehab.   "It works."

He followed her into the little office they used to count the money, one of four offices the minister used depending upon what mood he was in. Each office had a different kind of wall paper adorning it which the minister had carefully chosen to replace the painted walls his predecessor had left him. Fitswell found himself in the office that had pictures of ships at sea in its wall paper, all of them being 19th century and early twentieth century warships. *Probably had this wall paper installed to add some excitement to his obviously boring life,* Dick thought to himself.

A quick study, Dick Fitswell caught on quickly to the business of counting the church's money. In forty minutes they had completed the job. "Time to make my move," Dick decided, then prayed silently: *God, please do not let my dick get soft. I am your servant and my time of need hast arisen.*

Gloria wasn't up to his usual standards—he had fucked so many beautiful women. He had decided that first day he met her that his biggest challenge would be getting a hard on. Dick Fitswell immediately started thinking about someone else-------the woman he had fucked from the Country Western Bar.

"It's working. It's getting there," he said aloud.

"What's working or getting there?" Gloria asked.

"I don't know if you would understand," Dick replied.

"Try me. You might be surprised."

"I feel different than I've ever felt before. As if for the first time in my life I feel that I'm really part of something that's really meaningful," said Dick as he once again brought the moisture into his eyes hoping she'd see a hint of sincerity in them that he knew never existed. Dick had also practiced talking to his mirror so that using words like "I feel" became a part of his normal conversation with women. *Gets them every time*, he told himself. *Because most of them don't want a man who's really a feeling kind of guy....it's the words that get to them...Words that ring in their ears instead of their hearts. I feel. I like it..*

"I know what you mean, "Gloria replied. "I was like that when I first came here. I felt so lost and bewildered. I had felt that I had never done anything important with my life until I became involved here."

"I feel like that now," Dick said softly. "I feel like a boy again. As if life was suddenly renewed and bursting up out of me," he continued as he slowly spread his legs while still thinking about the blonde from the country western bar. As he spread his legs Dick Fitswell very subtlety cast his eyes downward in his bid to come off as being shy and modest. But he knew all too well how her eyes were following his and felt them boring towards his groin, seeing the huge bulge in his pants.

"I'm sorry. I don't want to offend you, Gloria. Since childhood I've suffered from a rare affliction. I get an erection whenever I feel overcome. When I get excited about anything. My doctor told me it's very rare. I'm embarrassed."

"Oh don't be. For a moment I thought you were thinking about something else."

"I wouldn't do that," Dick lied. "Not in church. But you are a very attractive woman. I didn't mean to say that you weren't."

"You really think so?" Gloria asked. "I haven't had a man tell me that in years. Or one who really meant it."

"Well, I mean it Gloria. And I did lie a little bit. I am very excited about being here. About counting the church's money with you. Something so important. But you have something to do with it too. I just can't help myself."

"Do you really mean it, Dick? Are you erect partly because of me?"

"I have to admit it, Gloria. And I feel terrible about this. It's just not right. Not here. Not our being in church. And while we are counting the money."

"Oh Dick. Please don't worry about it. If it happens it happens. I am sure that if God meant you to hide it He would have hidden it for you."

"It could be worse. If I was really concentrating my thoughts on you it would be much bigger. But I kept shaking it off. I kept thinking about God but as you can see it hasn't worked out all that well."
i
"Dick. There is no harm thinking about someone you find attractive. I am sure God meant it this way," Gloria replied as she looked at the huge bulge in Dick's pants and wondered what it looked like.

"Is it wrong for me to concentrate my thoughts on you?" Dick asked. "Here. In the ministers office?"

"I don't think it is. It is not wrong to think good things about others. Are you thinking good things about me, Dick?"

"I am and I will try. I am thinking about you now. You work so hard. You are so good. You are so selfless by devoting your time towards counting the church's money."

"I really try to be at my best, Dick. It makes me feel good helping others. Are you really thinking about me now?"

"Yes. Only about you. And I feel a warmness inside. You know how it is when you have a stiff drink. And you feel that warmth hit your body for the first time?"

"I know the feeling. I used to be an alcoholic."

"I feel that way now. And, I don't know how to tell you this." Suddenly Dick stopped talking knowing that the deliberate pause would effect her.

"Tell me what? You can tell me anything, Dick."

"Uhhhhh.......I am afraid to say it. My penis. It feels warm. For the first time it feels good as if a surge of energy has come over it. Something that is spiritual."

"Spiritual? In your penis?"

"Yes. Ever since I was going through puberty, I've been cursed by an overly large penis. It often hurts. Even when I'm not doing anything with it."

"I've never heard of anything like that."

"Gloria. I hope we can be friends and that you won't tell anyone about it," Dick Fitswell replied knowing all too well that she would and counting on it.

"About what?"

"My penis. Let me show you," said Dick as he slowly started to undo his zipper. "But we can't do anything here. That would be wrong. But I want you to know."

Within seconds Dick had whipped his penis out then shyly looked up into her eyes. "Now don't get the wrong idea. I just want to show you", he said as he stood up from his chair then laid his dick carefully on top of the table where they had counted the money. "See how big it it? I don't want you to think I'm a pervert or anything but I've measured it and it's eighteen inches long."

"That thing of yours is huge," Gloria explained. "You should feel lucky to have it."

"I am not lucky," Dick replied. "See that big vein there. It's much larger than it should be and my dick often hurts. It's a curse", Dick Fitswell lied.

Gloria had never seen a penis close to its size before. She was amazed at how knotty it seemed and how prominent the veins in Dick Fitswell's shaft stood out."

"Touch it Gloria. Right there on that huge vein. You will feel why I am so often in so much pain."

Gloria hesitated at first, then gingerly laid two fingers on the vein in Dick Fitswell's penis. Her fingers felt the blood course through the vein as Dick Fitswell became even more erect. Dick Fitswell's mind started to race: "I'm almost there. And it feels so good to feel a hand on my dick. Any hand. Any hand's better than mine."

"Gloria. That feels so good. Your touch is so tender. Do you mind if I put my whole dick in your hand?" he asked as he picked up his penis in his left hand and jammed it up into her palm. Gloria felt the involuntary stiffness start to well up in Dick Fitswell's schlong. She had never felt a schlong that large before. It's mere existence, and its being in her hand--her hand, caused tingles to ripple down her spine. She immediately started to get wet.

"Oh God. Make me stop," she called out as she tightened her grip on Dick Fitswell's penis."

"Gloria. We aren't doing anything wrong," Dick said heatedly. "If we were doing something God thought was wrong this would not be happening."

"I never thought about that, Dick", Gloria said as she started to jerk Dick Fitswell off. "It must be God's will then."

"He meant this to happen, Gloria. He ordained our meeting. Our being here. He wants us to do it in this office."

"There can be no other meaning," said Gloria as she put Dick Fitswell's penis into her mouth.

"Gloria. I don't think you could possibly be aware of it but your mouth. Your hand. Your very presence has healing abilities."

The sheer enormity of Dick Fitswell's penis in her mouth combined with knowing she was giving him a blow job in the minister's office continued to send ripples of pleasure down her spine but the ripples became an electro magnetic feeling that soon spread to her privates. Within two minutes of her first puttting Dick Fitswell's penis in her mouth, Gloria started coming. She had never felt anything like this before. Her mouth started to chatter as her legs went out of control, her body shuddering and shaking as her teeth tightened, then loosened, then tightened again into Dick Fitswell's swelled up member.

Dick Fitswell gently took her head in both his hands, then shook his head at her as he said, "It's wrong Gloria. Wrong that I come into your mouth. You must become one with me." Then he picked her up in his arms and carefully laid her out on the table. Thirty seconds later now undressed Gloria took Dick Fitswell's penis straight up between her legs. It took Dick ten minutes to come. After he shot his wad into her Gloria jumped up from the table. For a moment she felt dirty. Then she saw Dick Fitswell's ejaculate on the minister's desk mixed with what had just seeped out of her.

"Dick. Look what we have done? We have both come all over his desk. I think we should clean it up."

"It is good," Gloria. It is good that we both have come. I think we should leave it."

"You are right, Dick. Let's not clean it up."

"Wait a minute, Gloria. Get a towel. We are wrong."

As she was cleaning up the minister's desk with toilet paper she had found in the bathroom, Dick continued, "The minister seems to be a stick in the mud. We can't warn him about what we are up to."

"And what is that?"

"You feel good and I feel good. So what we have done is good. We should be spreading our joy throughout the congregation. Anything less is a selfish act. We cannot be selfish, Gloria, but I don't think the minister will like our doing what we have to do. That's why we cannot leave our come on his desk."

"I never thought of it that way, Dick. The minister really isn't any fun. It looks like it is up to us."

Dick Fitswell thought of that night four weeks ago that he had met Harry in the passenger car of the train he had used to escape from Canada back to the United States. Harry who was God or what Dick Fitswell thought God is. "Thank you Harry", Dick Fitswell said aloud as he lifted his eyes to the ceiling of his apartment. You have brought new meaning to my life and have made me realize how selfish I have been. You are right. I need to spread myself around. And only in giving of myself to as many as possible can I find eternal happiness in "The perfect fit."

Dick Fitswell makes his move on the minister's wife

Teaching Sunday school to a group of college aged kids was the hardest thing Dick Fitswell had ever done. *I've gotta keep my dick in my pants awhile longer*, he said to himself, feeling the cute blonde's eyes on him as he explained the next week's program.

At first the minister's wife came into his class with her husband who wanted to be sure that the new Sunday school teacher followed both his moral guidelines and his ideas of how and what to cover during class. Lately she had been coming in alone. *And I really can't blame her*, Dick Fitswell thought. *I am a lot more exciting than her nitwit of a husband.* Although he found that several of the young girls made him get an erection, it was the minister's wife he really wanted. Tall and slender, Linda had a model's legs and long blonde hair that flowed past her shoulders. Dick had a hunch that she'd make the perfect fit and even if she wasn't, he had decided that she was a far greater challenge and rewarding prize in the end than the tight butted college girls in his class.

He dreamed about her practically every night, fucking her as he dominated her-- slamming her head by her long hair into his mattress and nearly splitting her in half with his big cock as she lay there screaming. *I have to have her*, Dick said aloud. *The others will have to wait for their turn because if I bang them now, I won't have a chance with her.*

Dick Fitswell tuned the cute blonde out as he started focusing in on the minister's wife who had joined the class fifteen minutes ago. *She's impressed*, he thought smugly to himself. *And why shouldn't she be? I do everything well.* But it was time to say goodbye to the kids. As the last of his students filed out of the room, the minister's wife grabbed him gently by the arm.

"You really have a way with them," she said. "And you seem to have a firm grasp of the message of Christianity."

It was the opening Dick Fitswell had been waiting for. He had carefully rehearsed his attack, night after night, planning it well, making sure that it would all go as smooth as silk. He had decided that taking Linda by surprise was the most certain way of scoring with her.

"I don't agree with everything that's in it and what's being taught today by Christian churches all over the world," he told her.

"What don't you agree with?" she asked.

"I think we've lost the true meaning of what Christ was all about," he said. "Christianity as we know it is only concerned with getting money, about how much it can collect from everyone, and about how it can control millions of people so that it can get even more money out of them. Look at the early Middle ages when the Crusaders fought the Arabs because they had conquered the Holy Land. Think about that one. Over four Crusades just because the Arabs controlled the lands Christ was crucified in and look at it now. Calvary, where he was crucified, is now an Arab bus station and no one seems to know anything about it or cares."

"You can't be serious?" Dick. Are you trying to tell me that Christ was crucified in an Arab bus station. Are you crazy?"

"No. I'm not crazy. The cross stood right in the middle of what is now a street where the Arabs are parking and driving their busses."

"You are insane."

"Then let me prove it to you," said Dick as he opened the desk drawer from which he pulled out a thin paperback book. Dick had memorized the pages that contained the most compelling photographs to his case. He immediately went to the page that showed the old limestone quarry that the Israelites had started mining 1000 years before Christ during the reign of King David.

Only an idiot would believe that the quarry didn't resemble a human skull with empty eye sockets. And below the quarry was the Arab bus station.

Place in front of Skull Hill. This photo was taken by Author in 1950, before bus station, now there, was constructed.

"See that", Dick said heatedly. "That's Golgotha, the Place of the Skull where the gospels say that Christ was crucified. Call me crazy? Then tell me that quarry in which rains and weathering eroded cavities into the cliff isn't the place. That is Skull Hill. And those are Arab buses, not Christian or Jewish buses. And close by is the Garden Tomb which could very well be the real tomb of Jesus. And the only church which believes the crucifixion was here and Christ's burial nearby is the Anglican Church. The Church of England. The other Christian churches including the Roman Catholic Churches, the Greek Orthodox Church and practically every Protestant Church in the whole world have been selling their members a bill of goods, telling them he was crucified and put in a tomb around four miles from there."

"Let me see that book," Linda shouted as her face paled from the blood draining from her face.

Dick let it all sink in knowing too well that curiosity always killed the cat. For twenty minutes neither of them said a word as Linda rifled through the book's pages. The book, *The Search for the Tomb of Jesus*, had been written by William Steuart McBirnie,

80

PhD. His copy had been printed in Israel. Dick Fitswell had found it in a little shop owned by the Anglicans at the Garden Tomb in Jerusalem. He had walked all over the city looking for the Garden Tomb, hoofing it for miles and when he left it he was completely convinced that Jesus Christ, had he ever existed in the first place, had been nailed to a cross in what is now an Arab bus station.

Finally Linda broke the silence. "I want to borrow that book from you, Dick. I'll get it back to you next Sunday. You have no idea how important this is to me."

"Why is it so important to you."

"Because I have been to Jerusalem. My husband, our minister took me there. We were in the Church of the Holy Sepulchre for hours. We donated a couple hundred dollars to one of the churches there. A priest stood in the place believed to be the tomb of Jesus selling holy candles to practically everyone who came in there. We gave more than most."

"That's been going on for over 1700 years," Fitswell replied. "Priests and ministers selling candles, pieces of the cross, bits of the Holy shroud and other holy relics to pilgrims from all over the world. Millions of them. That's what I'm trying to tell you. That the Christian churches have been scamming everyone for centuries. Lying to them. Burning people at the stake who disagree with them. Expecting everyone to walk the holy line. Except it's not a holy line. It's a line of cow turds, horse shit and sheep dung."

"I'm going to read this book, "Linda replied. "And if it's what I think it is I'm going to read it many times. But Dick, what other reasons do you believe that Christ was crucified here instead of that other place?"

"First, and you will read about it in that book, at the time of Christ the Church of the Holy Sepulchre where practically everyone believes Christ was crucified and entombed was within the city limits of the Old Jerusalem. The Romans believed in leaving the bodies hang on the cross for hours and sometimes days after their crucified victims died. Now you and I are not going to believe for one minute that the wealthier citizens of Jerusalem would have put up with the screams of the dying not to mention their starting to smell in the hot sun as their bodies started to decompose.

"Second, St Stephen----well I don't consider him a Saint but the Catholics and Greek Orthodox do, was stoned to death near the bus station. The quarry furnished a large supply of rocks for all the stonings that took place in those days. They punished their "criminals" for the most part by either stoning them to death or by crucifixion. It would have made sense to have the execution grounds for both punishments close to each other. And the Church to St Stephen is close to the quarry and it says in that church that this is where he was stoned to death."

"Third—Both the Church of St Stephen and the bus station are right on the old road to Damascus, which was the most heavily used road in Jerusalem at the time of Christ. Stands to reason that the Romans would have wanted to make examples of executed "criminals" for the largest amount of people possible which would have been along a major thoroughfare."

"That would seem to all make sense," said Linda. "But I'm going to read this book and decide for myself."

"When you read it Linda, just consider this. At first the Roman emperors persecuted the early Christians but later on they decided that it would be better to join them than to try to continue beating them. After all.......by embracing Christianity they could better control the people. Not just physically but their hearts and their minds as well. And make a lot of money while doing it. All the better to find a place they could claim it all took place at. The death of Christ on the cross, then his resurrection from the dead. People would worship that place. Even kiss the ground where they believed the cross stood. So the Romans just happened to find the old wooden cross. Which was very convenient I'd say."

""My husband insisted we go to the Holy Land. I wanted to go to Hawaii. If what you say is true it would have been much more meaningful for me to have gotten a tan."

"Linda. We can talk about this later. When we see each other next Sunday I know you will be a believer. Right now I have to go home." Dick decided to break it off on his own terms before he had begun showing her the book. He wanted to feel on top and make her feel he was in charge. It worked for him on countless occasions before. And he knew it would work this time again.

She's mine. All mine. Next week I'm fucking her. There is no escape from the Fitz Express. Her husband is toast. Never liked the bastard in the first place.

More of Dick Fitswell's evidence on the Garden Tomb being the real place Christ was crucified

(which establishes Dick Fitswell as one of the leading Theologians of our time)

No...Dick Fitswell did not write the book that proves his points beyond a shadow of a doubt. But what he did was to cut through the bull by telling it like it really is which is that Christians have been taken for close to 1700 years. Just to solidify first the

84

Roman Emperors' then the churches' hold on their people who are all too willing to part with their money, their minds, and their spirit in exchange for giving their blind faith much the way that sheep do.

Through an exhausting journey on foot through Jerusalem Fitswell went alone searching for the truth. At last he found the real Golgotha and the Garden Tomb maintained faithfully by the Anglican Church (Church of England). Meanwhile millions of Christians continue to make their pilgrimages to the Church of the Holy Sepulcher where they happily donate their money to the priests and ministers within. As for the book---forget about buying it now since apparently it's out of print. We looked for it at Amazon.com. And found three other books by William Steuart McBirnie, but not this one.   Apparently it didn't attract the following it so richly deserved.

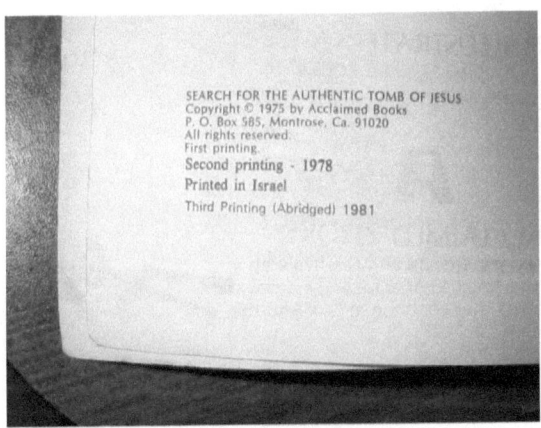

SEARCH FOR THE AUTHENTIC TOMB OF JESUS
Copyright © 1975 by Acclaimed Books
P. O. Box 585, Montrose, Ca. 91020
All rights reserved.
First printing.
Second printing - 1978
Printed in Israel
Third Printing (Abridged) 1981

But Fitswell, a pioneer and a legend got his copy, which had been printed in Israel and for a slight fee is willing to make reproductions. Fitswell also found through his scholarly studies that there is no other place in or around Jerusalem that resembles a human skull.

One of Fitswell's conclusions is that Christians were willing to kill countless Muslims during the Crusades starting around 1100 AD simply because they had occupied and controlled the Holy Land with the Holy sites but are now complacently content to let others do their thinking for them

Picture of the Biblical Golgothaat having an Arab bus station on the site of the Holy Cross because of stupidity, inertial and slavish devotion to the dollars that continue to flow into the Church of the Holy Sepulcher.

Aerial view of Jerusalem, 1935, showing (A) Probable execution ground of first century Jerusalem, The Garden Tomb, (D) The Damascus Gate.

Only a moron would fail to see that Romans liked crucifying their victims along a major road which in this time was the Road to Damascus. This major artery existed in front of the old city's gates and wound to one side of the Old Execution grounds where popular sports were held such as "Let's go get somebody else stoned" and "Let's nail the other guy".

In the new millenium a new era has arrived. In a field that has lost much of its original luster and justifiably so Dick Fitswell's future is as bright as any comet that has ever lit up the sky.

Dick Fitswell and the Ministers Wife

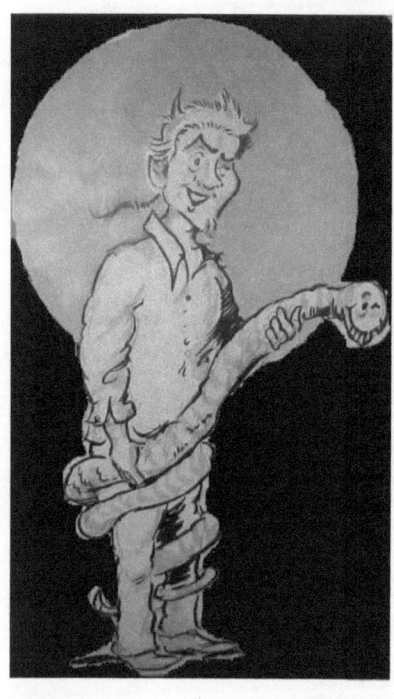

Once Linda started reading the book Dick Fitswell gave her, the minister didn't stand a chance. The facts were against him. Linda felt betrayed by her husband who had brought her thousands of miles to Jerusalem where the pair slogged miles through Christian religious sites. They had seen where the Last Supper was believed to have taken place. She had accepted the stations of the cross all along the Via Dolorosa as gospel. Her husband had taken her to all thirteen stations of the cross, along the traditional route believed to have been the one Christ carried his cross to Golgotha. She had wept at the Church of the Holy Sepulcher when she felt the spirit of Christ enter her as she looked upon the spot he was crucified in. But it was all a lie. Christ had not been crucified there. Fitswell had proven that. Instead, she had learned that an Arab bus station now marks the spot where the Holy Cross stood.

"Liars, imbeciles," she had cried out in her bedroom when the truth finally sunk in. "All of them. My husband who made me worship all those places where Christ did not suffer. And the idiot Christians who've been worshipping such false shrines for nearly two-thousand years and fighting over them for centuries. All of them blood sucking mental midgets. She immediately started divorce proceedings against her husband for mental cruelty.

She found Dick Fitswell just outside his Sunday School classroom saying good bye to his students while church was letting out. *Now there's a man who's not afraid to speak up for what's right*, Linda thought as she admired Fitswell's muscular physique.

"Dick, I read the book you gave me. You are right. I'm a believer now. You've probably heard I started divorcing my husband the day after you gave it to me. I just couldn't wait. I read the whole thing last Sunday night."

"You are very wise, Linda. To act so quickly without looking back. I'm proud of you."

"Can we talk? Privately? In the minister's office?"

"Sure," said Dick as he lead the way.

The sun was bright and the air was warm outside. Most of the church goers had left the church to go to Denny's or McDonalds but a few had remained to gossip just outside the church and most of the gossip was centered around the minister's upcoming divorce and as they asked each other *how could he ever be found guilty of mental cruelty towards his wife?*

*****

Linda's face seems uncommonly radiant, Dick Fitswell thought to himself as he watched her in the minister's office. *She's like an animal about to become unchained.*

Tall and thin---her figure at first glance seemed to be the prototypical model's body. But there was a lot more to Linda than what first caught the eye. Her very presence was electrical, leaving a sense of great physical strength, alertness, and agility

89

with the onlooker. Dick Fitswell had never wanted to fuck a woman as badly in his whole life.

"Dick. I want to thank you. Thank you for opening up my eyes to the truth", Linda said as she looked levelly into his eyes.

"Linda. I have a confession to make. When I first saw you, I thought I was looking at a wild horse, beautiful, and whose spirit was untamed but which found itself hidden away in a small corral."

"Funny that you should mention that, Dick, because I've often felt like bursting inside. Bursting to get out, to escape from the boring life I've had. All this energy just waiting there like a dormant sleeping giant."

Dick Fitswell moved close to Linda as he put his hands on her shoulders while looking into her eyes. "Linda. You and I were destined to be together and to meet here." Then he took her head gently into his hands as he grazed her ear lobes with his fingertips and kissed her. She opened her mouth just enough to let his tongue slide through, then sucked it back so that he could feel the vacuum.

Dick Fitswell had heard it all before. That all women are the same and that a fuck's a fuck. If he didn't believe it then, he certainly didn't believe it now. It started with a tingling in his groin. Then he felt a firm suction around his penis and that was when their bodies were not even touching. Only their lips. Her mouth was narrow with a firm tongue that he had noticed at church the first time she had spoken to him.

Stepping inside Dick Fitswell's legs, Linda put her arms around his hips and started squeezing which brought his groin tight up against hers. Five minutes later, he pulled away saying: "That's enough. I want you and you want me. Let's do it right on your husband's desk."

It took less than a minute for them to both get undressed. She tried to put his penis into her mouth but he waved her off, then

90

forced her down upon the desk as she spread her legs for him. This time Dick Fitswell didn't use any foreplay, telling himself, *I will impress her more if I just jab it right into her. She wants it and wants it bad.   Wouldn't respect me if I try to turn her on. She's already turned on.*

Dick Fitswell not only had a huge dick. He also had huge hands. As he thrust his pulsating member into her he covered her upper head with his hands so that the meat of his palms were over her eyes reasoning that she couldn't see. She couldn't see him and would imagine him as a huge ungovernable animal driving its huge penis between her legs.

It worked.   Linda started screaming, screaming louder each time he thrust into her.   And as she screamed he could feel her privates contract around his cock.   Then he remembered fucking the Chinese whore in Hong Kong and how he had fallen asleep dreaming of doing it with a vacuum cleaner. Only this was no dream.   She fit so tightly that each time he shoved his 18 inch prod into her he'd start to hurt, yet the pain was accompanied by exquisite pleasure. Unbelievably she kept getting tighter and tighter like a vice but not just an ordinary vice but a vice that kept sucking on his penis.

Linda's screams kept getting louder and louder.   At last Dick Fitswell started to come. As she sensed his being about to come she wrapped her legs around his back and started to squeeze. Dick didn't know it but Linda was a runner who attended gymnastics classes four times a week.   He felt like he was being squeezed by a Python as her privates literally sucked the come right out of him.   By the time they had finished his head was up against her neck with her long blonde hair flowing over his face.

His search was over--that hellish mission of finding the perfect fit. The elusive perfect fuck that had continued to torment him. Of always looking forlornly for a better conquest than those which preceded the latest one. Dick Fitswell was at peace with himself. But Linda's screams had been heard by everyone who was still in the church.

The first to run into the minister's office were Gloria and Fred who were counting the collection money in the room next door. Gloria---the woman he had fucked in the office only a few weeks ago, and Fred, a mousy little middle aged man who was being constantly badgered and bullied by his wife, Holly, who had ballooned up to over three hundred pounds by eating too much at far too many church buffets.   One of the rumors in the Church of Brotherly and Sisterly Love for Everyone was that Holly made it to nearly every church function just so that she could eat as much as she could. It was a large church that had many social functions and buffets, sometimes numbering as many as five a week.

Only seconds behind them was the minister, who rushed into the office, and seeing his wife naked on his desk with Fitswell on top of her, turned beat red.   The first one to speak up was Gloria who shouted at the top of her lungs. "How can you do something so despicable? And in the minister's office."

That did it. If there was one thing that Dick Fitswell wouldn't stand for it was taking sheep shit from a woman. Especially one that had been blessed by the full force of his semen jetting into her most sacred tunnel.   But it was the sight of the minister whose face was just beginning to flush with anger that angered Fitswell the most.

That fucking wimp. How dare him to get pissed off at my fucking his wife? Dick Fitswell nearly said aloud. But he had to deal with Gloria first who had committed number one error women must never make around him, which was being critical of his behavior which he now considered impeccable since finding out that he was the chosen one. It was he who had met God in that train car when he was escaping from Canada--not the minister, and not Gloria. And they had all been wrong to have taken their Christianity so seriously and to be so righteous over where Jesus was crucified, what were his exact remarks to Saint Peter and when. And so on, ad nauseum as had everyone like them for the past 1700 years. They were all sheep. Every last one of them.

"Shut your mouth woman," Fitswell said to Gloria. "Consider yourself lucky that I fucked you here. Most women in this church haven't gotten the chance. And I would say yet, but I've found my queen. Linda and I are going to be together for a long time. You've caught Dick Fitswell in his prime and you had damn better be proud of it."

"Get out of my office, you son of a bitch," shouted the minister. "And get out now. And take that whore with you."

If there was anything Fitswell hated it was men or women calling the women he fucked whores. After all, any woman lying down for a bout with his huge cattle prod of a penis, had showed impeccable taste by choosing him in the first place. Those who didn't were guilty of bad judgment in men and that's all that there was to it. Dick Fitswell fought back the urge to knock the minister down but moved a step closer as he put his face within inches of the minister's and said:

"Little man. Today is your lucky day that I don't just take your skinny little ass and throw you out your own window. But starting next week I'm taking over in this church and when I'm done with you the congregation's going to excommunicate you." Then turning to Linda, Fitswell said: "Let's get out of here. We have some serious fucking to do yet and then we have to get down to work."

Dick Fitswell takes over the Church

"My fellow sisters and brothers. I know we've not been together that long since I've joined this congregation. But I know you feel as I do that it seems we've all been close for eternity and it's eternity that's at stake here. Our very souls lie in the balance when we weigh the forces of darkness against the forces of light." Dick Fitswell paused for effect from the pulpit as he looked out into the hundreds of anxious faces of the churchgoers he now held in his sway. Then he continued, "You have been lied to by your minister but please put forgiveness in your hearts for he has been but a pawn in this travesty----this awful sin that has perpetuated itself upon Christians for over seventeen centuries. I have come from far away, appointed by a higher power, to reveal the truth so Let's take communion together."

Dick Fitswell was lucky to have two bartenders close at hand. Dick took out his pocket knife and cut a one inch gash into the tip of his thumb. Once the blood started flowing he put his thumb over each wine bottle as he squeezed it with his other hand. The cut was deep, deep enough to produce enough blood to color the once pale green wine a medium red, Fitswell's favorite color. Then he once again looked out at his new converts as the two bartenders prepared the communion glasses.

"This, my giving unto you my blood, is just one small measure of the enormous sacrifice I have made while finding out the truth. And my sacrifice is not complete yet," Dick Fitswell announced. "Come now and share with me my burden which will save you from eternal damnation."

They came in small groups of seven to twelve at a time to stand in front of the altar to receive their little squares of bread and wine. Each time Fitswell gave his people their bread and each man and woman washed it down with wine, a new group would replace the old until everyone had taken communion.

Three weeks later

"What is it exactly that we are doing here? Alice Breastready asked. "Other than having sex."

"This is very important," Dick Fitswell replied. All three of you have been chosen to spread the Holy Spirit. When we get done with our sacred mission in this office, I want each one of you to go out into the World and unselfishly spread the essence of Dick. Just as I am doing right now. Unselfishly as I commit myself to the good of humanity. And just follow my lead. This will come naturally to you."

Dick had moved a Queen sized bed into the minister's office a few days before. Linda, the minister's soon to be ex wife was already naked and lay spread eagled in the middle of the bed by the time Dick Fitswell had all of his clothes off. As he plunged deep inside of her, he called out to the other three women: "It was our destiny ordained by God Himself that Linda and I should meet. All my life I have searched for the perfect fit and now I've found her, which is more proof that together we are strong and have been called upon by God Himself to spread our strength to as many as possible."

Dick Fitswell never got tired of fucking Linda. As he rammed his huge appendage into her, he thought about how her lips would always suck his penis in, then grip around it like a vice. He had never felt anything like it before and would just as soon be fucking her all the time instead of having to put up with all the others who each in her own peculiar way turned him off. One of the women in the congregation, a twenty year old cute blonde college Sophomore, was just too loose. Another college girl, a leggy brunette, who had just turned twenty-one, talked too much while having sex with him. Then there was the thirty year old whose movements became too spasmodic while approaching her climax. "Acts too much like an epileptic," Dick Fitswell reminded himself.

"But I can't be selfish," Dick Fitswell told himself. "I have three more women to service. And that's just today."

He came in only five minutes as he vowed to somehow make more time just for her. Addressing the other three women, he said: "Crawl on up here with us now and take your clothes off. This next step is important." Eager to please, for after all, Dick had completely replaced the minister who Linda was divorcing, the three women soon joined them on the bed.

"Now I want you three to take turns sucking the come off my cock. And when it's all gone I still want you to take turns sucking me. That way I can recycle faster and get to each of you more quickly. For some reason having saliva constantly in contact with my member brings it into the mood quicker. Besides....I know you are all going to love my come. It's very rare stuff. Doesn't grow on trees you know. And the real prize goes to anyone of you who is lucky enough to get pregnant. You get a little Dick out of what is sure to be an ungodly experience.

When Dick was finished coming into Linda he repositioned himself so that he lay with his head and upper back up against the wall. Linda joined him, lying up next to him with her arm around his neck, as Alice Breastready lay between his legs and started sucking the cum off his penis, upper legs and lower abdomen.

Blonde, around five foot two, with a tight pretty little ass, Alice Breastready's greatest virtue were her succulent breasts. Long medium sized nipples that became easily excited were their crowning feature. When Alice finished rolling her tongue up and down Dick's shaft and after she had licked everything off his lower stomach and thighs, she pulled up a few inches which forced her breasts against his deflated shaft.

Linda watched Alice get down to business as she propped her head against the wall next to Dick's. Having just spent itself between Linda's legs, at first Dick's penis didn't respond. Then a little life came into it as Alice's tender moist lips gently sucked the come off it. But it was Alice's magnificent breasts which brought Dick back to life again. Her nipples started to pulsate after she rubbed them several times across Dick's shaft. Dick's penis, sensing Alice's now excited nipples, started to grow which made Alice shiver as she imagined 18 inches of belligerent cock shoved deep up inside her. Nipples tingling like crazy now, Alice started humping Dick's rapidly growing cock as she pushed it up between her breasts.

Linda watched Alice pass the point of self-control as she gloated to herself: "Look at that bitch thrusting her tits up and around Dick's cock, panting like a dog just hoping he's going to jam it up inside her." Alice was about to come. But catching herself at the critical moment, Alice asked:

"Linda. Can I suck your pussy as I get off?"

Linda looked down on Alice disdainfully, choosing her words carefully. "No, you can't. But you can lick all that cum off my leg. Just don't get your tongue in my pussy."

"Thanks Linda. I shouldn't have even asked. I should just be grateful that I am being allowed to lick all of Dick's and your cum off your leg. "

Alice greedily started to lick Linda's leg, savoring the taste of what Dick and Linda had jetted and oozed. She almost came right then and would have had Dick not stopped her. Still holding

Dick's penis between her breasts as she kept thrusting against him, with her nipples nearly having a voice of their own crying out-----"Now fuck me now", she stopped only when Dick shoved her aside.

"Now bend over, Alice, as I stick it in you from behind," said Dick Fitswell as he got ready to assume his favorite sexual position, while thinking to himself: "Puts me in the driver's seat as I dominate the gal."

Alice took Dick Fitswell's full 18 inches from behind as she imagined being totally dominated by a huge black Mexican fighting bull plunging its rampaging cock into her. Feeling Dick Fitswell's strong arms pulling her tightly against him as he thrust deep inside her, she came the first time on his tenth thrust.

Linda watched with a small self-satisfied smile on her face as she watched Alice continue to lose control. *Look at that bitch*, Linda said to herself. *Like a dog in heat getting it from behind and not being able to even look at Dick in the face. At least when I'm with Dick it is I who am in charge, willing his cock to come or not to come with a movement here or there with my pussy or giving him the right look as I pull his strings. I'm a goddess on earth.*

Dick shoved Alice's face into the bed as he continued to jam his penis up inside her, thrusting heavily as he pushed up against her buttocks. As he started to lose it, feeling hot come jell up inside he grabbed her tightly around her buttocks and pulled her tightly against his groin as he continued to pummel her face against the sheets. After he erupted and jetted his last drop into her Dick Fitswell yelled out: "Next."

"Come on Alice, get off that bed and let me at him," said Amy Snatchgood, who immediately jumped up on the bed next to Dick Fitswell, who was by this time recovering from having just fucked two women in a row.

Dick had carefully picked Amy Snatchgood to be one of his chosen disciples because of the fruit flavored smell emitted by her privates, which became even stronger and for him, more sensuous when she was having sex. The third woman with him was Teresa Tighttwat, who with her green eyes, blonde hair, and nicely shaped belly and legs was almost as good looking as Linda. Teresa patiently waited her turn, praying that her performance would be so spectacular that Dick Fitswell would forget about all the others.

Meanwhile a fifth woman lurked as she listened just outside the minister's office to the party that was taking place inside. It was Gloria, the first woman he had fucked inside the office, the woman who had been taking the collection money when he first started his ascension to the top in the Church's hierarchy. Dick Fitswell had not fucked Gloria since that first time right after he helped her with the collection money. She had not forgiven him either.

"So, I'm no longer good enough for your little religious ceremonies. Your precious fuck sessions. Well, we will just see about that," Gloria yelled out loudly as she opened the door to the minister's office and threw the Molotov cocktail against the wall next to the bed everyone was on as they watched Dick Fitswell putting it to Amy Snatchgood. Dick Fitswell had spread-eagled Amy, his third fuck of the day, out onto the floor and was busy humping her as Linda, Alice, and Teresa watched above them up on the bed.

Still in charge of the church's collections, Gloria still had access to the minister's office. A key was used to lock the door and this key could be used from either inside or outside the office. The Molotov cocktail was simply a plain vodka bottle that Gloria had filled up with white gasoline. She had then stuffed a rag into its neck after she had first soaked the rag in kerosene. When she had everything ready she quietly inserted the key into the door's keyhole. Then lighting the improvised wick Gloria opened the door to the minister's office, and threw the Molotov cocktail at the three women on the bed. It missed but it did exactly what Gloria wanted it to do.

Glass started exploding off the wall as white jellied gasoline spewed into the flame off Gloria's improvised wick. Stuff going

99

everywhere, up against the wall, on the covers of the bed, and all over the three women who were now busily watching Fitswell fuck Amy Snatchgood.

"Take that and shove it up your twats," Gloria yelled as she locked the office door from the outside. The bed spring and mattress were the first things to become engulfed in flames. The bookshelves and books lining them were to become the next. The three women didn't have a chance, becoming the objects of spontaneous combustion as the jellified white gasoline clung to their clothes and skin and caught fire as the bed beneath them erupted into flames.

Dick Fitswell immediately lost his hard on as everything around him burst into flames. .Somehow he was able to get Amy Snatchgood off the floor and close to the single window in the minister's office. Smoke was now filling the room. Dick Fitswell couldn't breathe or didn't dare to knowing the smoke would quickly asphyxiate him. With no time to lose Dick Fitswell threw his elbow into the window shattering the glass. Enveloping Amy Snatchgood into his arms Dick Fitswell hurled himself out of the inferno, landing one story below with Amy Snatchgood on top of him.

They lived to see the church burn to the ground before the fire department arrived. Dick Fitswell had a broken leg. Amy Snatchgood whose fall was broken by Dick's body was uninjured.

Dick Fitswell finds Paradise in the whorehouses of Thailand

"No more churches for me," Dick Fitswell vowed to the shapely Thai girl sitting next to him at the Bangkok bar.

"That's quite a story, the young prostitute said. "What did the authorities do to Gloria after she burned the church and killed those women?"

"Nothing," Dick Fitswell said. "She disappeared right after she burned the church down. When they searched her house, they found six dead bodies of men she had seduced. On the six o'clock news they were saying that she believed everyone of them had jilted her. They also found pictures of all her victims on her bathroom wall. My picture was on it with the others. She had rubbed shit all over each picture and I would probably have been her next victim. She's now on the nation's most wanted list, which is one of the reasons I'm here, Susie Chai."

"What's the other reasons you've come to Thailand?"

"Because I love fucking whorehouses."

Bangkok had over eight million inhabitants and this international Mecca for sex addicts was widely regarded to have a quarter million whores. The Japanese were renowned for targeting prominent Japanese business men for week long sex tours of the better known sex shows and brothels. At these sex shows a man could watch a woman having sex with a horse or a man sticking his prod into a chicken.

Although widespread throughout Bangkok the Patpong district was the most infamous of its sex centers.. Many of the Patpong bars resembled American topless clubs—to a point. A half dozen or more whores typically descended upon male new comers like vultures. The first time Dick Fitswell went into one of those

101

places, he found himself surrounded by six women while he watched a twelve year old girl masturbate with a candle on the stage. The girl on his right shoved her hand down the front of his shorts and started jacking him off as she asked him to buy her a drink. Not to be outdone, the girl on his left had pushed her hand up his shorts through its leg and started squeezing his testicles. A third girl gave him a neck massage while she kept jabbing her pointed breasts into his back as a fourth girl manicured his nails.

Everyone of them expected a tip. But he ran out of money after he tipped all of them. They kept on him until he emptied his pockets in front of them as if to say, "I'm penniless." Within seconds they deserted him as they prowled about the place looking for their next victim. Dick Fitswell wryly smiled to himself as he drank his beer alone as he thought about how he had kept only twenty American dollars in his pockets, after hiding five hundred dollars in his socks.

He found the Erection Zone on his third night in Bangkok. Walking through the place for the first time he commented to a West German sexaholic standing next to him, "This place is perfect. My Dick's going to fall n love." Dick Fitswell and the West German pervert stood in a gallery on the second floor peering through a large glass window at over thirty Thai women sitting in four rows, each girl wearing a numbered sign on her chest.

"I thenk I vant number seven," the German said to Dick as he continued to watch the women through a pair of Zeiss Ikon binoculars. "She has big teets."

"Naw. She's no good," Dick replied. I like number twelve. She's still wearing a skimpy g-string but look at that box on her. I'll bet she can really fuck."

"Some of zee vomen in zee gallery on floor number one vere vesser," The German said. Zoo young. I vill haf to say some are only ten years old. But you cannot fuck them from thet room. They are allowed only to give blow jobs. But they could be so tight. Just imagine."

Dick Fitswell had already imagined fucking a ten year old. For that matter he had once dreamed of screwing a goat and couldn't see much difference between the two. If there's one thing that could be said about Dick Fitswell, he did have morals and screwing children and animals was something he found completely reprehensible. He drew the line at eighteen year olds and if there ever was any doubt about a girl's age, Dick would ask her to show him her ID.

A Thai man in his early thirties stood a few feet from them dressed in a tuxedo. Dick had heard a lot about the legendary Thai bath and he wanted to get on with it. "I'll take number twelve," he told the man.

"What do you want to do with the girl?" the man asked.

"I want the Thai bath for forty dollars."

"Nothing else?" the Thai replied. "Don't you want to fuck the girl?"

"I don't know. I might," said Dick. I'll have to just see what happens. For now...just the Thai bath"

The man wearing the tuxedo let himself inside the gallery and approached the women sitting in their straight backed chairs. He had a thin white cane similar to those blind men use. The girl wearing the placard reading number twelve was seated in the second row. The Thai poked his cane at her chest as he said: "Number twelve, please. You have admirer"

The girl followed the man out of the gallery, then she watched Dick pay the man forty dollars. Dick turned to the German who was still watching the whores through his binoculars and said: "Big tits suck. Only a tight box that fits means anything to me. He wished the German good luck as he followed the girl into a special room where he would soon be experiencing a Thai bath.

This time the role of the sexes was completely reversed pitting Dick Fitswell, lying on his back on a little polyethylene swimming pool raft that had been positioned on a tiled floor, against his seductress, the young Thai whore he had just picked out. The little room was similar to a college dormitory shower room since it was larger than the typical shower found in many U.S. homes. But it had been built for an entirely different purpose. The room was meant to be filled with water from wall to wall to a depth of six to twelve inches so that the water would barely cover a man who was lying on the raft.

The Thai girl turned on a spigot which filled the little room up to a depth of seven to eight inches before she turned the water off. Slipping her bottoms off, she straddled Dick, hunching over him as she dragged her breasts across his chest, then his groin. Dick Fitswell's penis immediately grew to its eighteen inch fullness as he tried to pull her towards him. But the girl immediately jumped off him, wagged her finger at him as if scolding a child, and said: "You get Thai bath. Full treatment. Very clean. But you do as I say. No fuckee fuckee."

They had told him going in that the typical Thai bath or massage lasted a good hour and a half. Dick Fitswell resigned himself for the duration, fully aware that this time it would be the girl who would be in control. Dick Fitswell closed his eyes as he anxiously awaited the girl's next move. Feminine fingers started to play gently across his scrotum. Then stopped. He then felt them again, rubbing something onto his balls that felt like Vaseline. The fingers lingered there, taking a much longer time than would have been necessary just to rub ointment onto his testicles. Then he felt them move up to his shaft.

At first he felt them gently squeeze. Then he felt them knead the Vaseline like substance into his shaft. The girl's fingers quickened the pace as they started jacking him off in short quick strokes. Then feeling Dick Fitswell's mounting excitement the girl once against started rubbing his balls.

"Open up your eyes, Dickie," the girl commanded. As Dick Fitswell opened up his eyes the girl once against straddled him but this time she faced his feet as she stuck her ass up into his face. By the time she grabbed Dick by his ankles her privates were within two inches of his mouth. Dick Fitswell reached around the girl's

104

waist and started to pull her into his face. The girl fought back by letting go of his ankles, grabbing his toes instead, as she hunched down farther onto him so that his tongue still remained inches from her vagina.

Once again she reversed her position. This time she lay in front of him as she cupped his genitals with both of her hands and started sucking his shaft. Dick Fitswell never wanted to fuck someone as badly in his life. The girl kept changing positions. She would alternate between stroking his penis and sucking it. From tme to time she would squeeze more ointment into his balls. Sometimes she would just fuck his penis with her breasts after lathering them up with hot water and soap.

"What is your name?" Dick Fitswell asked the girl.

"Suzie. That is my name and yours is Dickie," the girl replied.

"I want to fuck you, Suzie. How much extra do I have to pay?"

"No fuckee now," Suzie replied. "You did not want it before. I make you come without fucking me."

"No. I want to fuck you. I will give you fifty more American dollars if you let me stick my dick in you," Dick Fitswell promised.

"No. Not this time, said Susie as she stuck her pussy right into Dick Fitswell's face while she put his dick in her mouth."

Dick Fitswell was amazed at how fit she was. She was tall for a Thai girl--nearly five feet eight and larger breasted than most Oriental women. Lean in the waist and stomach her muscles rippled as she got down on him. For the first time his tongue slipped into her opening, which is exactly what she wanted. Susie let Dick Fitswell grab her as he pulled her down onto his face. Then she pulled away, her face appearing totally detached as she put more ointment onto his balls.

I wonder how much longer I should let him go, Suzie asked herself. *I can make him come in two minutes or I can let him go*

*on for five. Or ten. It is all up to me. But I bet he is rich. So I will
not let him get everything he thinks he is going to get. He's going
to be mine for as long as I want him.*

Dick Fitswell had made his choice from among over sixty Thai
girls. There had been around thirty girls in the downstairs gallery.
Those were the ones who were not allowed to have intercourse.
Then there were the thirty odd girls from the upstairs gallery out
of which he had selected Susie. She was the most exquisite one
of them all. Longer legged and much more full breasted than
most of the others Suzie was still slender where it counted.
Moreover, she was very strong. As Dick Fitswell continued to
probe with his tongue up her opening he thought to himself:
Fucking her would be almost like fucking a lioness.

Without warning Susie once again jumped off of him. "No more
pussy in your mouth," she taunted him. "I make you come now.
Next time you will want more." Once again she mounted him, but
this time she sat on his upper chest so that she faced him as he
continued to lie in the little raft which was now completely
covered with warm sudsy water. She didn't need more of the
ointment to stroke his heated shaft. The hot sudsy water would
do just fine. Reaching behind her she once against started to
stroke him.

As she stroked Dick Fitswell's penis, she inched her opening right
up next to his face while she sat on his upper chest in order to
give him a good look. But her position kept him at just the right
distance. Her weight being firmly on his upper chest did not give
him the chance to force her bodily over his face. Dick Fitswell
could only watch her opening from inches away as he felt the
juices being milked out of him by fingers made slithery by the
combination of hot soapy water and ointment.

Dick Fitswell watched her opening oscillate as it got wider and
narrower. Susie had practiced making her pussy expand and
contract over years. She had shaved her pubic hair to give the
performance just the right effect. She had him—literally by the
balls.

"I will give anything for that pussy of yours," Dick Fitswell gasped.

"You can't have it now," Susie replied. "You are mine. You are coming and you have no control left."

He didn't. This time Dick Fitswell had no answers. As he watched her tight little pussy contract and convulse, he imagined himself inside her. Yet he could do nothing about it. He felt his shaft grow warm in her hand as the blood flowed along its entire length. As he finally stopped fighting her, letting go at last, he came and came, gushing through her fingers far longer than he had ever remembered. Susie pulled harder and harder on his shaft as she felt it get harder, then she watched dispassionately as it erupted and continued to erupt in short spasmodic bursts. After Dick squirted out his last drop, Susie Chai calmly raised her come filled hand to her mouth and started to lick it clean. Then shaking her head doubtfully, she said to him: "Not bad but I'm still hungry."

Dick Fitswell had completely lost control. He decided to do whatever was necessary to possess her. He started out by buying her out of the brothel and taking her to the nearest bar where he bought her a drink. Then he told her why he had left the Church for Brotherly Love for Everyone.

Dick Fitswell--taxi Driver in Bangkok

The four Americans leaving the Siam Royal Hotel had it all. Lots of money and the time to spend it on expensive vacations. Otherwise they wouldn't be at the Siam Royal Hotel where the rooms started at $250 a night. Let alone the fifteen hundred dollars per person airfare. Still----there were many less expensive options in Bangkok to the Siam Royal Hotel where a nice room could be had with a nice deck with a view and a refrigerator that had been stocked with four or five different brands of beer and more than half a dozen kinds of ready made cocktails. And for half the price. Dick Fitswell studied the four Americans trying to determine what had made them choose such an expensive hotel.

"Non discriminating, pig headed wives is one possibility," he reasoned. "The men have to know that many tour packages covering Bangkok or several entire Asian countries offer opulent hotel accommodations for far less. And they've been obviously pretty successful or they wouldn't be here in the first place. It's very likely that they've been goaded by their wives to keep up with the Joneses. Just to show off that they can afford to have the very best. And now the husbands are wanting to go off by themselves for a night on the town----their women no doubt too tired from a whole day's shopping."

Dick Fitswell had been on "such shopping tours" before in which the Asian tour guide got a cut out of the action. The bus load of tourists would be sold on the idea that the whole thing was a cultural experience. Each day the tour guide would instruct the bus driver to drive to several small factories which just happened to feature a little store selling whatever goods were made in the factory to the unwary tourists. Dick Fitswell had seen it happen many times before--in Hong Kong, in the People's Republic of China, in Korea, in Singapore, and now in Thailand. The tourists would be herded off to little factories that produced jewelry, dresses and other clothing, glassware, and even watches. Some of the operations were done by hand. Other operations by machines of every size and description. But in every case the prices charged at the outlets were much higher than one would have to pay in each city's thousands of shops. Whereas many of the shops selling the same goods could be found in futuristic malls that were a shopper's paradise, many others were located in outdoor markets selling the same items for a quarter the price.

The number one Asian shopper's paradise was Hong Kong, one of the three largest ports in the world, followed by Singapore which was the fourth largest—then Bangkok. One could buy practically everything in these cities, not to mention Taipei, Beijing, Manila, Tokyo, and many others. The latest Japanese sound systems, binoculars and cameras, jewelry, finely styled eyeglasses, to statues made of silver, gold, copper, and Jade. It amazed Dick Fitswell that so many American women bought more than half their stuff from the little factories the tour guides took them to. *Ridiculously unbelievable*, Dick Fitswell said to himself when they can find a much wider selection at half the price, in an air conditioned shopping center.

American husbands! What a bunch of pussies! Dick Fitswell thought as he remembered watching the greed on the women's faces as they went around the little factory outlets buying up everything in sight, eyes glittering, pulses accelerating as they moved rapidly throughout the stores looking through whatever merchandise was on display. *Stuff for themselves. Other stuff for the kids they had left behind in the States. Stuff for their mothers and their fathers and stuff for their friends. What a bunch of stupid fat pigeons, they are. And their husbands even worse, looking like a bunch of wet roosters that had all had their feathers pulled out.*

"They're mine," Dick Fitswell said aloud, as he gave the cab a little gas and pulled up next to the four men, all of them plump pot bellied guys in their late fifties or early sixties.

"Would you like a cab?" Dick Fitswell said to the men. "I know Bangkok like the palm of my hand. Can take you gentlemen anywhere. To dinner. For a show. For a good time."

"He speaks English like an American," one of the men said to his friends."

"That's because he is American, Joe. I've never seen an American cabby in Bangkok before. Let's take him up on it."

Dick Fitswell asked the men as they got into his cab, "Where can I take you?"

"We are not sure," said Joe. "We just had dinner with our wives. We are all out for a good time, if you know what I mean."

"Why aren't your wives with you now?" Dick Fitswell asked the men.

"Because they are too tired from that bus ride today."

"And shopping," one of the others answered.

"Okay, I think I got the picture guys," said Dick Fitswell. "You've come a long way and your wives are doing exactly what they want which is riding around all day long in a tour bus so they can spend all of your hard earned money. So you guys would like to do something on your own without them knowing about it. What would you think of having your choice of some of the most beautiful women in the world? What would you think of getting the most sensuous massage for just thirty bucks. One that lasts for an hour and a half? And getting to choose from sixty women for your masseuses?

"I think you are bullshitting us," the first man said. Then he extended his hand out to Dick as he introduced himself. "My name is Larry by the way. And yours is?"

"Dick Fitswell. And I'm always looking for the perfect fit. Good thing you guys ran into me. I'm just the man to get each one of you the perfect fit of your dreams."

"What are we waiting for?" said Joe. Take us to the place we can get massaged for thirty dollars."

It took an hour to get to the Erection Zone from the Siam Royal Hotel. Bangkok, a city of over eight million, was widely known for its traffic congestion. On the best of days it could take over two hours to get from one end of the city to the other. But all four men were anxious to go whore shopping, and Dick was lucky to find the traffic to be relatively light. It didn't take long after their arrival at the Erection Zone that Dick had them looking through the glass window at the women in the upper floor gallery. First he showed them the girls in the gallery on the first level, as he admonished the men, "But these gals here won't fuck you. At least not on the premises. They are only good for hand jobs and blow jobs. Me , I'd just as soon use my own hand. It's cheaper."

"Look at the gazunkas on that momma," Larry said excitedly. Dick noted that Larry was eyeballing a husky dark skinned Thai who was far bigger in the hips than he liked.

"I wouldn't fuck her on a bet," said Dick. "Putting it in her would be like sticking it in a toilet. Be about that loose and far dirtier."

"Who would you pick then?"

"I'd pick #12 there. She's tall and slender. And look at those legs. Not an ounce of fat on her and she looks strong. Bet she can squeeze the come out of you better than any woman here just by wrapping those gorgeous legs around you."

"She looks awfully sweet," Larry replied. "I think I'll take her.

Joe took a short thinly built girl. The other two men were quick about making their choices. As he watched "their new dates" escort his new companions to the tiled rooms that awaited them, Dick Fitswell called after them. "I'll just wait for you in the bar here in this place. You will need a cab home and I think I could use a drink."

Two hours later all four men were sitting with him in the bar. As soon as Larry came in, Dick Fitswell asked him, "She was more than worth it, wasn't she?"

"She was the best, Dick. I'm taking your advice every time from now on. I gave her my thirty bucks but by the time that hour and a half was over with I was begging for it. Finally she gave in and fucked me but I had to pay her a hundred and fifty bucks more. Man, was she ever tight. I'm seeing her again tomorrow.

"Why don't you guys get it again tonight, then still go back tomorrow, Dick Fitswell suggested. "When you get back to the United States you won't be able to come right back."

"That's a great idea, Dick," said Joe. "But this time I'm getting number twelve. Larry can get somebody else."

By the time the four men came back another two hours later, Dick was feeling pretty mellow. Eight beers at the special prices the bar was giving him had put him in a good mood. Not to mention the money he and Susie were making together now that he had turned cabbie. In the past four hours she had turned two tricks, collecting $180 from each man for $360. Out of that she had to give the Erection Zone its percentage. Still.....Counting what she had already made she had come off well. Plus Dick was getting a twenty percent commission off each dollar the men spent that went to the establishment's share and that commission also applied to drinks.

"Life is good, "Dick Fitswell said to himself. Got me a nice place living with Susie Chai. I'm meeting all kinds of interesting people driving a cab while seeing the city. I knew she'd fall for me as soon as I sunk my whole eighteen inches into her. And Susie and I are making a bundle. In a few months time we will have enough money to buy this place and then I can get on with pursuing my life's ambition--being a real Whore Master.

Dick Fitswell running the whore house

Spermutations was a dream come true for Dick Fitswell. "A whorehouse in Bangkok" is my destiny. It's me. It's what I'm all about," Dick Fitswell chuckled to himself as he sat in his office with his feet stretched out on his desk watching "his girls" slowly filter in to work their shifts on the twenty-seven inch monitoring screen he had installed. On it he could watch every room in the place. Horizontal and vertical lines on this screen subdivided its surface into twenty-four zones which he could watch simultaneously. Nine little rooms where the girls and their customers did the Thai baths, the Spermutations bar, the dressing room, and even the parking lot were under Dick Fitswell's scrutiny along with the five "Fuckee Fuckee" cubicles. Most customers started with the Thai bath as they enjoyed the one and a half hour massages but invariably ended up paying more to copulate with the girls. Some preferred getting on with their business in the Fuckee Fuckee cubicles as soon as the bouncer asked them what service they wanted. In the long run such experienced customers paid less for the penetration they longed for while others simply didn't have the time to go through

113

the hour and a half long Thai bath. The display was on a timer which showed each zone for two seconds, before going back to the overview screen which showed all twenty-four zones simultaneously. Then it would go to the second zone, return to the overview screen, before going onto the third zone, and so on. Dick Fitswell had a mouse which he could use to click on each individual sector of his display which would temporarily interrupt the automatic processing of the images by bringing up whatever room he wanted to view full size.

Dick Fitswell clicked on the lobby. Each girl had to pass through the lobby to get to the dressing room. In the center of the lobby was a life sized Dick Fitswell statue, poised like a Greek hero in the nude with its eighteen inch penis at a full erection. Dick Fitswell watched a girl pause before passing the statue, bow her head, and kiss the statue's penis.

"Atta girl," Dick Fitswell said to himself. "Now bow down to the floor." Dick Fitswell watched the girl bow down at the statue's feet in the reverent manner that Asians seem to have a monopoly on.

Another girl followed the first one into the lobby. Dick Fitswell noticed her lips barely touch the statue's penis. Then he watched her bow, but the bow was nothing much more than a curtsey. "Goddamn Bitch," Dick Fitswell almost screamed aloud.

Dick Fitswell reached for the intercom, speaking authoritatively into it after turning it on. "Outside, in the lobby," Dick Fitswell's voice boomed. "I want that last girl in my office." Within a minute the girl was standing before him after being escorted in by his bouncer.

"What's your name?" Dick Fitswell asked the girl.

"Tila Hungchow," the girl replied.

"Sounds Chinese?"

"I am Chinese Thai," the girl replied.

114

Dick Fitswell leaned back in his chair and lit a cigar—an Anthony and Cleopatra, a long narrow oblong cigar he favored not so much for its taste but because it vaguely resembled his penis. "Do you like your job, Tila?"

"Yes. I make lots of money here."

"Then why don't you show me some respect around here? Why don't you kiss my statue's penis with love and affection the way the rest of the girls do? Why don't you bow down to it and SHOW ME that you love me. Show me that you see me as the father you wished you could have had."

"I am so sorry, Mr. Fitswell. I have a bad week. Forgive me please. I do better next time."

"I'll give you another chance. When you finish your work I want you back in my office before you leave. You can go now."

A third girl came in just seconds after Tila left his office. Tall for a Thai, the girl was much more curvaceous than the other girls he usually saw in his place. Large pointy breasts jutted out from her t shirt. Dick Fitswell had never seen her before which was not that unusual since his bouncer did much of the hiring. Dick Fitswell spoke into the intercom: "I want to see that girl in my office."

A minute later, the girl was standing before him. Once again Dick Fitswell stretched his feet out onto his desk as he puffed from his cigar. *They need to know in no uncertain terms I'm completely in control and they're not,* Dick Fitswell thought to himself. *I have to show them that I really don't give a shit about them.*

"You are new here, aren't you?" Dick Fitswell asked the girl.

"This is my first time, Mr. Fitswell."

"You've been briefed about what you must do then? And about my rules?"

"Yes, Mr. Fitswell. I know what to do."

"Good. See me here in my office when you are done."

*****

Fifty-seven girls worked their shifts in Spermutations that evening. Out of the fifty-seven, Dick Fitswell had seven visit him in his office when their shifts were over. The tall girl with the prominent breasts was the sixth.

"I've just penetrated five of your coworkers," Dick Fitswell told her as soon as she came into his office. "My dick is starting to ache. I want you to make it well."

"Me no understand," the girl replied.

"Me, stickee, fuckee five ladee," Dick Fitswell told her as he pointed up five fingers.

"What you want me to do?" the girl asked.

"Suck on it," Dick Fitswell said as he pulled his zipper down. "Go down on me now," he ordered her as he pulled his appendage out. "Smokee me now."

What's one more? the girl thought to herself as she kneeled down between Dick Fitswell's legs and put his penis into her mouth. *I've just fucked five men. But it beats doing the dishes at the local Thai restaurant.*

Dick Fitswell's penis was nearly raw from all the hard use and had taken on a red color. Worse, his balls had started to ache. But as the saliva from the girl's mouth started to drench his shaft he once more started to get erect. "Suck my balls for awhile," he told the girl, making sure that his voice displayed enough firmness.

Dutifully the girl obeyed, after tenderly lifting up his enormous dick to give her free access. Gently licking his scrotum, she

116

proceeded to put each testicle in her mouth. *One at a time*, she thought to herself, *but not so long that he will become bored. I have to become one of his favorites.*

That's where they belong, Dick Fitswell thought, *Servicing my needs as they prostrate themselves right between my knees.*

Dick Fitswell was running out of juice. It took him twenty minutes to come, right between the girl's teeth. But there were only a few drops of semen in his stream. "How much did you make tonight doing the extras?" he asked her.

"Five hundred dollars," she replied.

"Give me four hundred and fifty dollars. Then I'll let you go." He didn't bother to search her as he collected the money. "You are getting ten dollars for working your shift. Sixty dollars is more than enough to feed your family."

By the time the seventh girl arrived in his office, sex was the last thing on Dick Fitswell's mind. There remained—only his ego. *I have to fuck her,* Dick Fitswell vowed to himself as she walked in the door. *She needs a lesson, right up the ass.*

"Tila," Dick Fitswell addressed the girl. "Listen up and listen closely. Next time you go by my statue I will be watching and I expect you to lick the statue's dick with love and affection, then lie down at its knees and kiss its feet."

"Yes, Mr. Fitswell. I not do again. I will do you honor."

"You'd better or you will be a street whore doing it for the stray dogs that can't afford this place. Now, let's get down to business. I want your tip out. How much did you collect from your customers?"

"Six hundred," the girl replied.

"Give it to me," Dick Fitswell ordered. I don't have much time."

After she handed him the money, Dick Fitswell grabbed her purse and went through it.

"Okay then. You aren't holding out on me. But I'll have to strip-search you. Take everything off. Now. Then I want you to stand with your back towards me."

Twenty seconds later, Tila stood with her back facing him, completely naked. Dick Fitswell started at her ankles, moving his hands up her long legs. He fondled her buttocks. Sliding his hands around her he probed her vagina with his fingertips before bringing his hands up to her breasts. At first he cupped them in his palms, then he grabbed both nipples at the same time and squeezed them hard with fingers of rigid steel. Tila gasped from the sudden pain and tried to jerk away. Dick Fitswell grabbed her roughly around the waist which jerked the ninety-five pound girl snuggly against him. Then he stuck three fingers up her ass. Tila screamed in pain as Dick Fitswell searched with his fingers for currency she might have harbored there for additional take home money. Suddenly he said to her: "You are never going to have it this good."

Dick Fitswell reached into his desk drawer and pulled out an electronic pump up and a jar of Vaseline, then ordered the girl, "Bend over."

Trembling the girl bent over Dick Fitswell's desk. Sticking his right hand in the little jar, he grabbed a thick glob of Vaseline in his fingers and rammed the messy jell up her ass. Dick then plugged the pump up into a near by AC receptacle and turned the little appliance on after putting it around his scrotum and the base of his penis.

It was not the normal pump up if one could ever call a pump up normal in the first place. This one was run by electricity. Dick Fitswell lit another Anthony and Cleopatra as he relaxed to the soothing vibrations of the little machine. His penis had turned from a red hue to a black and blue tint with a sickly yellowish cast. But the little machine was magic, because it not only brought him to a full erection it also elongated his eighteen inch penis another five inches. He poured himself a glass of scotch, took a healthy swig, and set the half empty glass on his desk.

Tila screamed as she took the full twenty-three inches up her anus. Dick Fitswell twisted her body so she was facing squarely away from him as he thrust her face down on his desk. As she collapsed across the desk Tila's stomach grazed the half empty glass of scotch and spilled its contents across the desk onto Dick Fitswell's penis. The liquid spewed onto the electronic pump up and seeped into its wiring which the manufacturer, a fly by nite outfit in Hong Kong, had not taken the care to ground. As the pump up shorted out Dick Fitswell felt the jolt of electricity grab his scrotum and penis like a vise of sharp razors. The room was filled with a sizzling sound as smoke started to pour out of the contraption. Dick Fitswell felt the pain for only a second or two before passing out.

Dick Fitswell's Useless Appendage

Dick Fitswell came out of the coma fourteen days after his electronic pump up shorted out on hi . *I had this dream*, he said to himself as soon as he reached a barely conscious state, *that I had the perfect fit.* His memory had come back faster than his doctor thought possible. He remembered a beautiful, willful Thai girl with firm pointy breasts skewered on his large penis, squirming and screaming as she tried to escape from his relentless, throbbing pleasure stick. *Right up the ass*, Fitswell style, he nodded in approval as the memory came back to him like an apparition from the past. He remembered the pump up and how six whores in a row had sucked the come out of him. He remembered how he didn't think he could get off with this seventh girl, the most beautiful and enticing of them all and his having to rely on the pump up. He vaguely recollected blanking out as indescribable pain coursed through his penis and scrotum. Dick Fitswell slowly opened his eyes and saw the IV stuck in his arm.

"My penis," he screamed aloud, so loud that they could hear it outside the room, that booming Fitswell voice, a cry of anguish that reverberated throughout the entire third floor of the hospital. "It hurts. God it hurts. I must check it. See if it's all still there." Dick Fitswell reached into his hospital gown with his left hand and grasped his appendage. It was not even semi erect. Just a flaccid misshapen object he had never felt before.

"It's not mine, he yelled out. "It can't be. They must have sewed this thing on." Scared shitless over what he might find there or not find, Dick Fitswell pulled his hospital gown off which left him naked under the surprised eyes of the nurse who stood riveted in place while tending to the patient next to him.

"My pubic hair's missing!" he screamed as it suddenly dawned on him that only singed stubs remained from his once glorious bush.

For the first time in his life Dick Fitswell felt the onslaught of uncontrollable panic. *I have to know*, he thought to himself, as he started to jerk himself off, *if this thing's ever going to work again.* But the erection never came. He only felt a limp gelatinous mass squirming between his fingers.

Susie Chai heard Dick Fitswell's screams from the waiting room and ran into the room just in time to watch her man nervously jerking his schlong. She silently watched unobserved as Dick Fitswell tried to get it up. For a full fifteen minutes she quietly watched him beat off but his once proud member remained as flaccid as a limp balloon.

When Susie Chai rushed into Dick Fitswell's office at the Spermutations Club she realized she had to do something and do it quick. She immediately smelled burning flesh and hair, and then she saw that his penis had shriveled down to a blackened tinker toy still attached to the electronic pump up. The last Thai girl, the girl who had failed to properly bow down to Fitswell's statue, was still in the office bouncing around the room, her face beaming.

"Crispy critters," the girl kept shouting out. "Fitswell critters. He's finished now. Leave that thin little stick to the termites," she told Susie Chai in Thai.

Dick Fitswell's Anthony and Cleopatra cigar still glowed in a heavy cast ashtray that had been shaped into two testicles with a large dick between them. Grabbing it with one hand, Susie Chai struck the girl across the bridge of her nose. Blood spurted from the girl's face seconds after Susie heard the satisfying crack of bones breaking from the blow. Susie watched the whore collapse to the floor.

A whore herself, Susie Chai knew practically all there was to know about the nuts and bolts of a man's sexual apparatus. Although as a city of over eight million, Bangcock had several good hospitals, Suzie knew the best hospital for genitalia malfunctions and disease was the Chunk Dong Hospital in Beijing, China. She had Dick Fitswell's inert body heliported from Bangcock's

121

International airport to Beijing where he was immediately airlifted to the Chunk Dong Hospital.

Nothing was spared in the expense of resurrecting Dick Fitswell's penis. The funding for the Spermutations Gentlemen's Club had all come from Suzie who had made her money through honest toil and sweat while lying flat on her back in the whorehouse. Although Dick Fitswell had done well as a cabby bringing customers to the whorehouse along with tips and kickbacks along with money earned from selling drugs to foreign tourists, he had squandered it all in a neighboring whorehouse, the Slippery Dick Saloon. He had been the establishment's leading customer which had soon changed its name from the Eruption Zone to the Slippery Dick Saloon in his honor. But Suzie Chai didn't seem to mind, figuring what was good for the goose was good for the gander. As one of the most beautiful women in Bangcock she had a wide selection from some of the richest men in the world.

For Suzie Chai Dick Fitswell was a dream come true. The fact that he cheated on her several times a day was a turn on. Suzie Chai had no use for men whose behavior she could easily predict. She avoided serious relationships with the wealthy because she was afraid of losing her independence, and she despised nice guys as chumps she could easily take advantage of. And even though Dick Fitswell was the biggest Dick in town by the time he got to her place he had already fucked so many girls that he usually arrived dull and listless. Even worse, by the time he got home his penis had been worn to a frazzle. What had started out as the best fuck in her life had become an endless series of unfulfilled sexual encounters.

But a bright light shined before her. *He'll shape up*, she constantly told herself while the constant memory of that first time she had experienced his full eighteen inches loomed in her memory. She often thought of his sticking it in hundreds of other women and saw him as a wanted man—a man women would compete for and whom some of them would even die for even though she couldn't think of a single reason why they'd want to. She just knew they would.

Watching Dick Fitswell's futile attempts at bringing himself to an erection made Suzie Chai feel as if she had finally united with him, in body and in spirit. She was carrying his child but had not gotten enough nerve to tell him and was waiting for the right moment to bring it up. *Dick needs me*," she told herself. *Now more than ever. I will make him well. And if he ever regains the use of his penis I don't care how many women he fucks or loves as long as he fucks me once in awhile.*

Dick Fitswell couldn't get an erection and passed out. Suzie Chai motioned to one of the nurses.

"Get me Mr. Fitswell's doctor. This is very important," she explained to the nurse.

The nurse disappeared for a few minutes, then returned to Dick Fitswell's hospital bed with a doctor. Dick Fitswell slept on dreaming of a guillotine decapitating his penis. Eighteen inches of erect Fitswell cock lay stretched out in the cutting groove. On the side where the basket that was normally used for collecting heads a ravishing blonde with succulent breasts kneeled clasping his penis as she stretched it through the groove. The blonde was laughing, taunting him, as she played with a rope, which would trigger the heavy blade's descent upon his shaft. Ashen faced, Dick Fitswell sweated profusely as he watched the blonde play with his penis. Rubbing his head between her palms at first, then stroking his shaft, the blonde alternated back and forth as Dick's hard on became an erect steel spear.

Suddenly she started speaking to him. "See this rope Mr. Fitswell. This isn't an ordinary rope. I put it around your shaft like so. The rope had thin monofilament fishing line attached to the free end. The blonde tied the monofilament line around Dick Fitswell's shaft just behind the head then pulled it tight. A few inches above her head was a pulley. Reaching up the blonde adjusted the pulley so that there was no slack remaining in the monofilament line or rope.

The blonde could have been American or German, but her voice was Asian. Her breasts were crowned with long tapered nipples, made erect and firm by the excitement building up from her anticipating what was to come. She stood up and turned around to show him her back and buttocks. Dick Fitswell took in her thin waistline and fine ass which flared outwards into lines of perfection such as he had never seen before.

"As you can see, Mr. Fitswell, I am the perfect woman of your dreams. Think of me as----"The perfect Fit. But you can't have me. I have your manhood in a death vice. As you can see, the line is tight, almost as tight as my pussy. You are so fond of your big penis, aren't you, Mr. Fitswell? Right now you are at your full eighteen inches but when you loose your erection it will pull on the line. And when it has pulled just several inches it will trip the blade...and...Too bad Mr. Fitswell. This will be the last erection you will ever have."

Outside the dream the doctor and Susie Chai discussed Dick Fitswell's predicament. "Spare no expense Doctor. He must go on to fuck again. No one else is like him." Suzie handed the doctor fifty one hundred dollar bills, and added. "Do whatever it takes. There is more if you make it work again for me."

The blonde once more crouched next to the Fitswell in the dream, this time on the other side of the guillotine. Up close......she pushed her breasts into his face. Suddenly she pulled away, then pried open his mouth with her hands as she inserted a nipple. "Suck deeply, Mr. Fitswell. Think of me as a mother like figure. Not a real mother. More like an anti mother. I am not here to give you life but to take it away. When your penis is dismembered and as you hear it flop into the basket you will start to bleed to death. There is no one here to save you Dick Fitswell."

The guillotine was not like those they used in France during the French revolution. Back then its victims had to lie down on their stomachs. The blonde had Dick Fitswell sitting down with his legs outstretched in front of him with his hands tied behind his back. She continued to tease him with her breasts. Then she mounted him. Dick Fitswell had no choice but to look up her privates. But he didn't want a choice. He didn't have a choice. His tongue suddenly went out of control as it probed upwards licking her labia. The blonde bored down on him to give him greater penetration. Dick Fitswell closed his eyes as he tried to imagine what it would be like fucking her.

The blonde arched her back as she came in Dick Fitswell's mouth. When she finished she said: "Now, Mr. Fitswell, it is time for you to come."

Going over to the other side of the guillotine, the blonde lay on her stomach as she took Dick Fitswell's penis into her mouth. At first she drew it slowly between her teeth, then she quickened the pace. Dick Fitswell was about to come for the last time. Sensing it the blonde took his shaft out of her mouth and stood up. She came over to Dick Fitswell's side of the guillotine and took one of his balls into her mouth while gently letting her tongue caress it as she soaked it in her saliva, before moving onto the other testicle.

When she sensed that his excitement was at its zenith, she got up one last time and went over to the other side of the guilloteen where she once more started to suck on his shaft. Moving quickly, she continued to draw it back and forth in her mouth until she sensed he was about to come. Then for the last time she took his shaft from her mouth and bolted over to the other side a final time.

"Goodbye Mr. Fitswell. Enjoy your death," she taunted as she took his right ball into her mouth. Only a few seconds had elapsed from the time she had been sucking his shaft. Dick Fitswell had been only seconds away from coming. The blonde's soft moist mouth continued to titillate him. Dick Fitswell felt the warmth flow up his penis as he started to come. Feeling the sperm gush out of him the blonde crunched down onto the testicle with a vice like grip. At the very height of his climax Dick Fitswell felt her teeth drive through his flesh. He kept coming as his body quivered uncontrollably. White sticky ejaculate continued to cascade out of his penis.

In the past, Dick Fitswell had been able to keep his erection up for an hour–two hours at a time. He had fucked girls, left his dick inside of them, kept it hard and fucked them again without losing his hard on. But not this time. His orgasm was complete. He had spent his last drop. As the excitement faded so did his hard on. Violent pain from sharp teeth penetrating his sack permeated his consciousness as he started to lose his hard on. By the time his shaft had shrunk to ten inches the line was pulled just tightly enough to trip the hair trigger spring the blonde had set up next to the pulley. He heard the blade come down. Three-hundredths of a second later the blade descended onto his shaft and severed it.

Dick Fitswell screamed out in agony as he watched his blood spurt his life away. The blonde had kept her face six inches away from his penis when the blade struck, already fingering herself as the blade severed his shaft. She had timed everything perfectly, her orgasm hitting its peak as his life blood squirted into her face.

Outside the dream the sleeping Fitswell started to scream. Alarmed, Susie Chai and the doctor studied Dick Fitswell's inert body. His flaccid shaft was shrunken. A large glob of come lay next to the small penis.

"I want everything done for him that is possible," Susie Chai told the doctor, visibly shaken by what she had just seen. Fitswell had screamed in his sleep and come all over his bed, yet his penis had showed no signs of an erection. "And I want you to put him under psychiatric evaluation," she shouted to the doctor. "And as soon as possible."

126

Dick Fitswell meets Howie the Duck

Swan lake

Mr. Fitswell, I want you to meet Dr. Kwan," Dick Fitswell's Chinese doctor announced as he gingerly guided a Chinese woman in her early thirties to Dick Fitswell's bedside. "I've done all I can. I've repaired all the burnt and cut tissue on your penis. It's taken a month. We've had you in physical therapy but I'll be very honest with you. Your dick still doesn't work and I don't think it's going to work until you have gone through some very extensive psychiatric therapy and even then all we can do is to hope for the best."

"What do you mean, hope for the best?" Dick Fitswell asked the doctor. "It has to work. I won't be a man without my penis being fully functional at its 18 inch limit." Dick Fitswell studied Dr. Kwan, carefully noting her slender build, long raven hair, and ferret like eyes behind glasses that gave her a studious look. *She'd be a goer alright. With the right man plugged into her*, Dick Fitswell noted.

"I need a few weeks with you," Dr. Kwan said. Months perhaps. It all depends. You might get it up again. Then again, you might not. That's going to be determined by the success of my psychiatric therapy."

"That's going to depend upon whether or not you take your clothes off, what's underneath, and how you use it," said Dick Fitswell.

"Enough," Dr. Kwan announced. Then turning to Dick Fitswell's doctor said, "Dr. Peters, I need to be alone with Mr. Fitswell in order to conduct my first psychiatric examination of his condition."

After Dr. Peters left Fitswell's bedside, Dr. Kwan pushed a button. Two large robotic hands of polished aluminum retracted from the hospital bed, snaked around Fitswell's arms, found his wrists and clamped around them as two other mechanical hands grabbed Fitswell's ankles. Fitswell couldn't move. Dr. Kwan carefully removed the plastic bag that the hospital used for IV liquids and fastened a new bag to the apparatus.

"Don't worry Mr. Fitswell. It's only Sodium Pentothal mixed with a sedative," she said gently as she jabbed the IV needle into a vein in his wrist. You will tell me in time everything I need to know. The Nazis called this truth serum but our stuff is even better. You are going to tell me about your childhood, what kind of women you like, what turns you on the most, how, when, and how many times you masturbate and what your biggest sexual hang-ups are"

Within fifteen minutes, Dick Fitswell was reduced to a very calm almost comatose sack of human jelly as the IV started to work its magic. Dr. Kwan moved over close to Dick Fitswell's face.

"Mr. Fitswell, I believe you had your first sexual experience in your early teens. Tell me about it. How did it happen?"

Dick Fitswell felt very tired. Dr. Kwan's voice was deep and resonant, barely feminine at all. He could not lie to it, believing that if he did he would never be able to go to sleep again. "I was eleven," Dick Fitswell started off. "I lived on a farm in West

128

Virginia. My father had a still on our farm and we didn't have many neighbors back then."

"Please go on," said Dr. Kwan. "I am very interested."

The nearest city of any size was over fifty miles away and the nearest town was seven miles from where we lived. That is where I went to school. My Dad didn't believe in having a television set. There really wasn't much to do on that farm. Until that afternoon when we finished bailing hay. Being only eleven, my dad didn't expect me to put in a full day's work. Not even close. It was a hot afternoon and I had gotten pretty tired. There was a pond not far from that alfalfa field where we were bailing so I just went over there to cool off and get a little rest. And that's where I saw that damn duck."

"What duck?" asked the psychiatrist.

"Howie the Duck. The same duck who became famous."

"I do not understand," Dr. Kwan replied.

"I went to the pond but started to take a little nap before going into the water. Suddenly I woke up. At first it seemed as if I was dreaming. There was this big duck and it was fucking all the female ducks. I watched it fuck one, then another, until finally it had fucked ten female ducks in a row. Then it looked back at me. And the duck said: "You haven't seen nothing yet. Watch this." That duck started to fuck another duck, then pulled out and started giving it to another one. Then it flew off a short distance and brought two more female ducks with it. I swear that duck lined those four female ducks up and kept going from one to another until it had fucked them all."

"Sounds like he was a very special duck to me," said Dr. Kwan.

Dick Fitswell continued. "Suddenly all the ducks disappeared. But the next day I went out into the chicken coop to get some freshly laid eggs. And that duck was in there fucking all the female chickens. But that's not the half of it. After I watched it fuck over

129

half a dozen chickens, the duck turned around to me and said, "Dick, want some?"

I said: "Want what?"

And the duck replied: "A nice juicy chicken around your meat. See if you can make one of them squawk."

"No thanks," I told that duck. "My Dad might find out and then with my luck he'd probably make me eat the chicken."

"I saw the duck again the next day. We had this large mongrel dog. Half German shepherd. I heard my dog outside the farm house squealing as if it was in pain so I went outside and there was that duck again, fucking our dog."

"Then what happened?" asked the doctor.

"Damn if that duck didn't get off that dog when he got finished, came up to me, and said: "Sorry I haven't introduced myself properly to you yet, Dick. Name's Howie. Howie the Fuck Duck. That's what a lot of barnyard animals call me."

"My name is Dick Fitwell," I relied to that duck. "But my daddy calls me Dickie."

"Well Dickie. Why don't you just follow me to that pond. There's something there that I think you will really like."

"What? Please tell me," I replied.

"The most beautiful thing on earth. Trust me," Howie said as he gave me the most benevolent smile that I've seen on either man or beast."

"So what did you find in the pond?" asked Dr. Kwan.

"There were two swans. Both female. Howie approached one of them as he looked back at me with a mischievous grin, then said,

"I've got this one. You can take the other. I've left you with the prettier of the two."

"I watched Howie stick it in the swan. She tried to get away but Howard held her tight. Then the swan, which was much larger than Howie, tried to fly off with Howie still stuck in her. That damn duck just swatted that swan right across the face. Really smacked her good which made her immediately calm down so Howie could finish fucking her. But before he finished he looked at me again and said: "Whenever you are dealing with a female let her know who's boss right away."

Then Howie got off the swan, looked at me and said: "Your turn Dickie. Let's see what you've got."

"So did you do it?" Dr. Kwan asked.

"I sure did. After all, I had watched Howie fuck enough animals. By then I knew exactly what to do. I just pulled my pants off and snuck up on the other swan. Then I grabbed her around the throat and just stuck it in her. It took me awhile to get hard but I somehow managed to get it shoved in just part way. That swan was ready."

"What was it like?"

"She was tight. I think I hurt her a lot. As I said, I got it in just part way and then the swan started to struggle. She started flapping her wings and about beat me to death but the more she struggled the harder I got. It was exciting. Damn exciting. When it was all over I was black and blue all over but I managed to ejaculate into that swan in the end. Made me feel like a real man."

"I'm surprised you didn't get killed."

"I almost was which added still to the excitement. After awhile the swan started to fly away. Here I was stuck deep into that swan and she started to take off. Which really got my dick swelling. She started to fly across the pond low over the water. I just hung on as I continued to pump her. We must have gotten around half-way across when I came. I was only a little boy then. No where near the man I am now. I had no staying power so as soon as I came I started to get soft, mydick came out and I just kind of fell off—right into the water."

"So you didn't get hurt other than black and blue?"

"No. It was great. Tightest fit I ever had. And when I fell into the water I just swam to shore. Didn't even have to clean my dick off. The water did it for me."

"What happened to Howie?"

"He waited for me with a big grin on his face. Then he took me out drinking."

Dick Fitswell has his first Woman

Dick Fitswell was beginning to see the Chinese psychiatrist as much more than his doctor. For the first few days of his therapy his dick hung below his belly limp and useless. During the nights after falling asleep he'd ejaculate in his hospital bed as he dreamed on. Dreams from his past came to him—dreams about a childhood half-remembered that he'd just as soon forget. As each day passed his flaccid member slowly became more alive. Chinese physicians had been able to restore the tissue damage the electrical short in the penis pump up had inflicted, but the psychological damage had remained. Dick Fitswell's once proud eighteen inch penis had died and so had its owner. Life had no meaning for the man who had lived the never ending quest for the perfect fit. But his psycho therapy sessions with the young Chinese woman slowly brought his dick back to life. Dr. Kwan had become much more than his doctor. She had become a sexual object worth despoiling.

"What happened to Howie the Duck?" Dr. Kwan asked.

"He taught me everything I needed to know about sex," Dick Fitswell replied. "At first it was the swans. But after we had fucked a few they started to grow wary. They'd fly off every time we came near that pond. Finally they flew off never to return. But a flock of geese visited the pond so we screwed several geese, but the same thing happened that had happened with the geese and they left too.

"Then what happened?"

"Howie introduced me to sheep, then goats. But all of them caught on to us and they would run off as soon as we came anywhere near them."

"And what did you learn from all of this?"

133

"I learned to get very aggressive because if I didn't, I'd never get laid."

"When did you have your first woman?" Dr. Kwan asked.

Dick Fitswell frowned, then his face brightened. "I had just turned twelve. Howie the Duck was still around, but by that time we had run out of animals and he had started to get restless. Dick Fitswell's voice started to sadden as he recalled his last adventures with Howie the Duck.

"I had this sinking feeling that Howie would soon leave me so I asked him: "What are we going to do, Howie?""

He looked at me with this funny gleam in his eye and said: "How about trying a woman?"

"Where am I going to find one of those?" I asked him.

"Haven't you noticed the girl next door? What's her name?"-----------Howie paused for a moment----------then continued, "Cathy. Cathy."

"But she's only eleven."

"Are you blind? She's ripe for the butcher. Her breasts are just starting to develop. Her nodules are just beginning to blossom. She's perfect."

******

The young Dick Fitswell knocked on the door of the neighbor's that stood out by itself less than half a mile from his parent's farmstead. A few moments later a little girl with a ponytail appeared. "Hi Dick—I was just doing my homework for school. It is so boring."

"How would you like to come out and play?" Dick asked her.

"Come closer so I can get a better look at it," Dick Fitswell said as he sat on a slab of concrete that was part of the abutment supporting part of the trestle. Kathy sat down next to him, still marveling at his penis.

"I wish I had one of those," she said. "It's much bigger than mine."

"Let me show you something else," Dick Fitswell replied to her. "Touch it."

Surprised and curious Kathy gingerly touched Dick Fitswell's penis, then she pulled her hand as abruptly away as if she had just fondled a snake.

"No. Touch it again and keep it there." This is really neat. You aren't going to believe it."

Kathy touched his penis again, just as gingerly as she had the first time but this time she left her hand on it. Dick Fitswell's penis started to grow. "Feel it growing as you touch it. Hold it tighter in your hand and pull it back and forth. Let's see how big it is," Dick suggested.

Kathy was fascinated by how Dick Fitswell's penis expanded in her hand. *What other new things is he going to show me?* she thought as she pulled on his appendage.

"See, how big it's gotten?" Dick Fitswell crowed. "Keep working it back and forth while I show you something else."

"What's that?" asked Kathy.

"Your thing. Let me touch it and feel it."

"I don't know. My daddy told me to never let a boy touch it."

"That's because your daddy is afraid that you will feel good and want to do it all the time with everyone. Trust me, Kathy. You've

136

liked what we are doing so far. You are going to like this even better," Dick Fitswell replied as he touched her between her legs.

"It feels good," said Kathy. "It's really kind of exciting. I'm touching you and you are touching me. This feels so good."

"Well if you like this, let me show you something you will even like better."

"What's that?"

"I'm going to put my thing into your thing. If you think this feels good, you will feel much better and even more excited when we do it."

"I don't know. I think this feels good enough."

"Kathy, don't you want to do something even more exciting. T his can be our little secret. No one else has to know."

"So you had sex with her then? Which makes Kathy to be the first woman or girl you ever had intercourse with? What did you think of it?

"I was really surprised," Dick Fitswell replied. "And disappointed. Kathy wasn't nearly as tight as the swans or the geese. But by this time the swans and geese had disappeared so I didn't have any choice. Kathy was all I had so we kept going out to the trestle to fuck. I just didn't have anything better to do."

"Then what happened?"

"She got pregnant. Her parents sent her away so she could have the baby. She was only twelve when she had it. They had a little talk with my parents and I was whisked off to a boarding school. Place had only guys. And it was far from home."

*****

"Look at this thing!" Dr. Kwan. I've gotten hard. Just thinking about fucking all those swans and geese, and then Kathy, has made my penis come alive again."

"Let me take a look at it," Dr. Kwan replied. "Pull it out of your gown."

Dick Fitswell pulled his dick out which had reached a full ten inches. It was the greatest moment in Dr. Kwan's career. Her psychotherapy had reached its pinnacle. Out of the ruins of a nearly deep fried penis she had pulled off the impossible. Dick Fitswell had gotten his first erection. It was not necessary for Dick Fitswell to say a word. She had to test his penis herself........just to be sure it was fully functional. Grasping Dick Fitswell's shaft Dr. Kwan stroked it gently, at first out of curiosity, then as it slowly sprung to its full eightenn inches in her hand, out of professional pride.

"Dick, we've done it!" she exclaimed. "I think it will work. You might be cured."

"Might be?" asked Dick. "Then we have to find out. Let's take it for a test spin."

"Why not? It's late at night and the nurses have gotten lazy since most of the patients are asleep. No one will bother us at this hour."

Dr. Kwan crawled under the sheets with Dick Fitswell and buried her head between his legs. She had never experienced eighteen inches of raging cock in her mouth before. She started giving her patient a blow job out of sheer professionalism at first, in the sincere belief that she must not leave a single stone unturned before she released Dick Fitswell from the hospital. She had to have basic empirical data that his penis worked and there was only one way to find out and that was to test it. It would be necessary to find out that not only could he get it up but that he

138

could keep it hard in a woman's vagina until intercourse was completed. Premature ejaculation was not an option.

Dick Fitswell's huge member throbbed in her mouth. She found it tasteful, not acidic the way many of her sexual partner's had tasted because of the improper diet they were getting. The hospital food had been meticulously prepared for Dick Fitswell to be properly balanced in every respect. Dr. Kwan resisted the urge of having him jet his come into her mouth, as she reluctantly released his organ from her mouth. Then she turned over on her back and spread her legs for him.

There was still a little light on just above his hospital bed which showed off Dr. Kwan's body to him. She was long legged for a Chinese and tall with a flat belly. Her breasts, typical of most Asian women, were small but hers were well shaped with firm little pink nipples. Dick Fitswell plunged right in, at first inserting his penis only part way. Then as he felt her excitement grow he slid it halfway into her opening. Which was a lot further in than she was used to. Or any woman for that matter. Moments later Dr. Kwan lay beneath him quivering in ecstasy as nine inches of excited cock explored her orifice.

Unable to contain himself any longer, Dick Fitswell jammed the full eighteen inches of his organ deep into her cavity. Dr. Kwan gasped with the sudden pain, then she grasped the little support rails on both sides of the bed in both hands to brace herself against the Fitswellian onslaught that she knew had barely begun. She felt as if she were about to explode as the huge appendage kept ramming into her. Dick Fitswell had not had sex for weeks other than those times he had leaked semen onto the hospital sheets as he dreamed about past sexual exploits. Unable to contain himself any longer, he rammed his last inch deep between her legs and thrusted violently against her. What had been searing pain for Dr. Kwan became an interlude of indescribable excitement as she contemplated the very real possibility of membranes and tissue being torn apart by Dick Fitswell's relentless cock.

The whole thing only took ten minutes. Feeling what seemed to be a powerful animal violating her, Dr. Kwan reached behind Fitswell and plunged her fingernails into his back. When he started to come, she exclaimed: "Do it. I want it all. Keep pushing." Dick Fitswell pounded her body mercilessly with his chest and legs as he exploded into spasm after spasm of jetting ejaculate.

Dick Fitswell was cured.

Erectile Fitswell Saves Holland

FITSWELL
SAVES
HOLLAND

"But is he really cured?" Dr. Kwan asked herself as she watched Dick Fitswell pump the sheets the next night. This time he didn't get an erection and when he came his sperm wimped out on him in short underpowered spurts that would have gotten him laughed out of a convent.

He's reverting again, Dr Kwan noted in her memoirs, which she had entitled My most unforgettable fucks. *I need that driving cock inside me again guided by his animal mindlessness. I want the beast pummeling me. I have to have him because he doesn't give a shit about whom or what he fucks. I need to make him well-- to make him whole again so that I can feel him reaming me while he's exploding inside me.* "Dick," she silently prayed to herself, *I want to feel that huge piston of yours inside me and the thought of you not caring about me as you inject me full of your precious fluids.*

She couldn't sleep that night but the next day a solution came to her. *I need to shock him. Have to come up with something that will remind him of his past that will really piss him off. Only then can I force him to release that animal passion lurking in his subconscious. And hopefully, this time, my cure will be long lasting.* But that was the doctor in her reminding her of how she had taken the sacred Hippocratic oath that admonished all doctors to look after the welfare of their patients above all other considerations.

On a baser level a little voice kept telling her: *I need to make him need me. So that I will become indispensable to him. Only then can I always count on good sex. When he looks at me as the only way he's going to get it up and come he will be mine.*

*****

That night she brought to his hospital bed a photocopy of a painting. Dick Fitswell looked at the photocopy, narrowing his eyes as he studied it. Then he lost it, bellowing, "That is not what happened. For hundreds of years the Fitswells have been deprived of the recognition that they deserve. I hate history. It's made up by a bunch of fucking liars."

The photo copy was of a famous painting of the Blue Boy saving Holland by sticking his finger into a dike which kept the low lying Holland countryside and towns from flooding. The painting depicted the Blue Boy as a town idiot, the kind of fool that would have gladly volunteered to be shot out of a cannon.

"That is not what happened!" Dick Fitswell exclaimed. "My great ancestor, Erectile Fitswell, saved Holland as only a true hero could. He should have been revered and immortalized forever. Instead, he was forgotten!"

"What actually happened?" Dr Kwan asked calmly.

"My ancestor, Erectile Fitswell, was the first great man in the Fitswell clan. He was born with a huge cock but he suffered from poor eyesight since birth. Which was the best thing that ever happened to Holland until the Germans invaded that swampland during World War II. He tried to fuck everything in sight. So he was a lot like me. But being half blind a lot of ugly women had a chance with him. Legend has it that he really made the rounds."

"You've had hundreds of women yourself, Dick. Any idea, and I mean we'll never actually know the exact number, but have you any concept of how many women Erectile Fitswell fucked?"

"No one knows for sure but it had to be in the thousands. Thousands. I have proof of that because it is a known fact that the average Dutchman has a seven inch penis whereas the average man only has six inches. Erectile impregnated a lot of women back then. Since he couldn't see worth a damn he started to get bored since all the women looked pretty much alike to him. And the more bored he got the hornier he became as he started visualizing himself in all kinds of bizarre sexual situations."

And that's what did it. Dick's bringing up his ancestor being in bizarre sexual situations, not to mention the name itself, Erectile Fitswell. Dr. Kwan's mind went into a dream like state as Dick Fitswell's voice continued. The event----Erectile Fitswell's saving Holland with his huge cock became as real as watching the History channel.

******

At six foot seven, Erectile Fitswell was tall for a Dutchman in the old days. His height made him conspicuous enough. But his seventeen inch penis was something he wanted to keep under wraps until he had to use it. Since he was fourteen he had gotten into the habit of using a leather harness his father used for the horses to strap his cock to his leg. But today it had gotten very hot and the heat had made his leg sweat underneath the leather strapping. Perspiration started to seep down his huge holster which got his cock tingling.

"I need to fuck someone fast,"Erectile Fitswell bellowed. "And I need a hot bitch. One that won't peter out on me after just a few minutes of my dick!"

He saw the dyke just a few meters away but because of his poor eyesight he hadn't noticed that she had been there for a good while, watching him. The woman had a reddish cast to her skin, was around seven feet tall and was very broad in the hips.

143

Erectile couldn't be sure but he thought he saw a greenish liquid oozing out of her. "Aha, he exclaimed triumphantly, "it must be one of those lesbian bitches I've heard about. There's very few of them around. They used to burn them at the stake."

Erectile Fitswell remembered how his father had once told him about witches and how one could always tell a witch from a normal woman. "They will often have seeping from their genitals a discolored fluid that can be yellow or green. Sometimes it is red although one can easily mistake a menstruating woman for a witch when there's a red discharge present," said his father. "And take my word for it. A lot of witches screw each other. I've often wondered what it would be like fucking one of those kind of witches. But I've never had the chance."

It was the chance of a lifetime. Erectile's father had never fucked a dyke before. And never even met a witch. "Forget the preliminaries," Erectile shouted at the woman. "You want my cock and my cock is sweating up a storm wanting to release itself into your hole. Stand aside, woman as I introduce you to the best cock in Holland."

Within seconds Erectile had torn off his pants, not even bothering to undo his belt. Taking off the leather harness was a different matter since all the sweating had made it stick to his penis. Carefully peeling off the leather strap, Erectile had the gnawing feeling that somehow the dyke would run off and leave him, naked out in the field. But she patiently waited for him to finish unlimbering his huge member, still oozing that greenish watery substance that proved once and for all that she was indeed, a witch and a woman who preferred other women to men.

By the time Erectile Fitswell got his cock ready for action the oozing had become a torrent, a virtual stream of liquid gushing out onto the ground. "She wants me," Erectile said to himself. "She's so excited she's already coming all over her own legs. "I haven't a moment to lose," he shouted, as he plunged his penis deep inside her hole.

Fucking the dike was like nothing he had ever experienced before. As his dick expanded into its opening Erectile felt a wall harden around his shaft that refused to yield. "It's a dyke," he shouted excitedly. "It's a dyke and I'm fucking her so hard she will never have anything to do with another woman again."

But it turned out to be the other way around. The dike was made of stone masonry which is the reason Erectile's penis failed to sense any give in the hole he was fucking. Had he not been so excited he would have noticed that shoving his shaft back and forth in that hole was like fucking sand paper. His penis started to bleed into the hole of the dike just as he started coming.

Several local farmers found him stuck to the dike with his penis still inside it. Erectile Fitswell had passed out from the loss of blood.

"Look at that idiot," one of the farmers said to the other.

"But look at the hole in that dike. If he hadn't started fucking it it would have gotten bigger and bigger. In no time the whole dike would have burst and all our fields and crops would have been flooded. Most of Holland would be under water right now. That man's a saint."

*****

"So what happened to him?" Dr Kwan asked.

"They put him in an insane asylum. Some gratitude, huh? Erectile Fitswell saves the whole fucking country and they reward him by putting him in a nuthouse."

"So did he die there?"

"He got leprosy. Then he died. But before he died I am proud to report that he fucked all the female lepers in the place. He was truly a great man, always thinking of others, giving a lot of pleasure to all those lepers before they passed away."

145

"Well.....he was obviously a little more than crazy," said Dr. Kwan.

"No he wasn't," said Dick Fitswell. "He was just half blind is all. But I'm pissed off right now from just thinking about the raw deal he got. Turn over. I'm fucking you in the ass."

For the first minute having Fitswell's eighteen inch cock up her ass hurt. But it should have hurt a lot more. In fact, her whole anal area started to get numb as Dick repeatedly rammed his raging penis into her tight opening. Dr Kwan started to feel a peace she had never felt before. *I am needed,* she told herself. *I am here to cure him and to be an outlet for his rage. I must sacrifice myself to this great man.*

Dick Fitswell explains why Henry VIII beheaded his wives

"You are not cured yet," Dr. Kwan lied to Dick Fitswell, as he lay on top of her with his big 18 inch cock plunged deep inside of her. "I still need to know if you can successfully copulate inside of me while you are thinking about other things. Today's test is for you to tell me about another one of your ancestor's sexual exploits while you maintain an erect penis while fucking me.

"Let me tell you about what really happened to King Henry the Eighth and his six wives," said Dick Fitswell. "And how back in the 16th century, my great ancestor, Gonad Fitswell, changed the course of human history. It all started when:"

Henry stood in front of a suit of armor he had been admiring. The royal armorer had set thirty suits of armor in the Tower of London's East Wing. Out of these Henry was to choose one as the model for his personal custom armor which the armorer would build according to Henry's specifications. Completely nude while he studied the suit of armor in front of him, Henry thought about how he always got a hard on whenever he fought in battle watching the enemy knights dressed in armor of every description. Mounted vertically on little platforms the suits of armor gave the impression that each one was inhabited by a knight. Henry noticed how the suit he was admiring had its arm raised upward holding a long sword as if it were a knight about to slash downwards on his enemies.

"This is the suit for me," Henry said to himself. "It's giving me the biggest hard on of all." Like an irrepressible little boy Henry then made the biggest mistake of his life when he grabbed the armor's other mailed glove and started to shake while speaking to the suit: "Thanks a lot old buddy. I'll never lose a fight wearing an outfit like yours." Henry was over six feet tall and had a firm handshake. The suit of armor started to shake. Henry never saw the heavy long sword fall out of the mailed gauntlet as it fell across his erect penis. Before the sword hit the floor, it had whacked off the head of Henry's penis.

Henry's palace guard found him screaming on the floor in a pool of blood and summoned his physician immediately. Luckily for England the physician was able to stop the bleeding. Henry's chief advisor, Cardinal Wolsey, was on the scene in minutes.

"Henry's never going to be able to fuck again," the physician told Cardinal Wolsey.

"This is a devastating blow to the prestige of the crown and England's reputation," Cardinal Wolsey exclaimed. We gotta do something and we have to do something fast. History's not going to regard Henry as any sort of a man unless we can find a stuntman."

Ten thousand soldiers scoured England looking for one and found him in a pig sty screwing a slut on a bed of straw. Gonad Fitswell was the King of England's double. Best of all, he had a thirteen inch penis.

The first of Henry's wives Gonad Fitswell had to service was Catherine Arrogant. A staunch member of the Catholic Church, Catherine never enjoyed sex, and always insisted on Henry's shutting off the lights when he banged her. She never noticed the difference between the "new" Henry and the old one when he came into the bedroom. And didn't notice that the new Dick was thirteen inches long while Henry's had been a much smaller nine inch woman prodder.

Whereas Henry usually snored up a storm, Gonad Fitswell never snored at all. Catherine had gotten used to Henry's loud snoring and had found it soothing enough to lull her to sleep like a long forgotten lullaby. But Catherine had developed an acute case of insomnia ever since she had started sleeping with Gonad. One night it finally dawned on her that Gonad was not King Henry and she yelled out to him: "You motherfucking prick. You an imposter. Get out of my bed."

Something had to be done. Henry applied to the Pope for an annulment from Catherine since Catherine had been his father's widow. When the pope refused, Henry said to Gonad: "Fuck the Church. We'll start our own church. We will just call it Henry's Church."

"Better call it the "Church of England," Gonad replied. "Then they won't blame it all on you."

The new Church of England annulled Henry's marriage with Catherine and the pope immediately excommunicated King Henry who by this time had Gonad Fitswell banging his second wife, Anne Boleyn. "Who gives a fuck about the Pope," King Henry told Gonad. You are screwing more women than anyone in Italy and my army can outfight those Italian cowards anytime."

The problem was that although Anne Boleyn had given Henry a female child through Gonad, who was later to become Queen Elizabeth, she had not produced a male heir to the English thrown. Henry confided in Gonad: "That Anne's a real bitch, not giving us a boy child. We need to get a new woman, Gonad. For all I care she might turn out to be a Joan of Arc which is good enough for the pussy French, but we are Englishmen after all, and Elizabeth isn't going to look very cool riding around in a suit of armor.

So they had anne beheaded on trumped up charges of treasonable adultery. Henry's third wife, Jane Seymour, died during childbirth. King Henry and Gonad now chose Anne Cleves as Henry's fourth wife but when they found she wouldn't drink with the guys, Henry divorced her.

By this time Henry had become a fat fuck. The years had taken their toll and like a castrated animal, he had become corpulent. Gonad Fitswell, now in his fifties had likewise become a bloated remnant of his former self. Years of alcohol abuse had gotten the best of him and his once proud member had shrunk to six inches. Marrying Catherine Howard, a twenty year old palace tramp, Henry hoped to recapture the glories of his youth even if it meant having Gonad do his fucking for him. When Henry's spies told him she was screwing all the palace guards, Henry got drunk with Gonad.

"She's fucking around on you, Gonad," Henry told his friend.

"Which one of them is?" replied Gonad Fitswell.

"Catherine. She's turned into the palace whore and that's hurting my reputation."

"Not Catherine!" Gonad Fitswell exclaimed. She'd never want to fuck anybody but me."

"Well she is," said King Henry "and we have to do something about it."

"Come on Henry. She's still a good fuck."

"Hey Gonad brains—a big dick you once had but it's a good thing you were never king because your mind has always been smaller than your penis. The reputation of the crown of England is on the line here. I need to keep my reputation as a stud intact."

"What are we going to do then?"

"Off with her head. Just like we did with Anne. That always solves all the problems with women."

There was to be one more wife for King Henry. They say, she made him good coffee in the mornings. She was also a lousy fuck which didn't matter anyway since Gonad Fitswell's penis had by then shrunken down to only four and a half inches. Gonad Fitswell died at the age of fifty-five from alcohol abuse while Henry lived to be a very fat old man

"That really pisses me off, said Dick Fitswell. Even without half his penis King Henry the eighth came out of that story as a stronger character than Gonad Fitswell. What a disgrace to my name. I'm getting out of this Chinese dump and going to strike out on my own and create my own History. Besides, Gonad Fitswell only

had thirteen inches. World....get ready again for Big Dick."
Fitswell angrily jetted his semen into Dr. Kwan who hugged onto him forlornly, thinking: "I've lost him. What have I done wrong?"

Dick Fitswell celebrates Christmas

"I am so damn glad to be out of that Chinese fruit farm and away from that Dr. Wacko", Dick Fitswell said to himself as his plane arrived at the San Francisco airport. I am back in the U.S. just in time to celebrate Christmas. "Fuck Christmas. If it wasn't for my Dick Fitswell Fund to help the homeless I'd just sit this sorry ass excuse for a holiday out." Dick Fitswell pondered the real meaning of Christmas for a moment as he lusted after his blonde stewardess's shapely ass. "There are more suicides on Christmas than in any day of the year," he remembered from reading an article in *Time Magazine* several years ago. Think of all the families barely making it being railroaded by beady eyed merchants into buying all those presents they couldn't afford. Of mothers and Fathers dreading each new Christmas knowing all too well they are going to be put months behind in paying the bills all because of those rotten Christmas carols being played on the radio, those Christmas lighted displays in all the stores and people going around ringing Christmas bells all crying out in unison: "Give, Give, give to the kiddies or be a smuck". And look at all the depressed people out there because they never got married, don't have a steady boyfriend or girlfriend, or because they got divorced and no longer have custody of the children as they remember Christmases past when the whole family could get together. *I'm sure glad I am doing something about it*, Dick Fitswell thought smugly to himself.

The sidewalks of San Francisco were filled with the homeless. Here it never got below 55 degrees. Which made the city a Mecca for homeless people of every description–men and women, clad in light jackets, with only a sleeping bag or a blanket or two for a shack. They covered the sidewalks like roaches. Dick Fitswell moved among them, every now and then picking someone at random he would give a hundred dollar bill to. He had been doing this for ten years, each Christmas heading for the streets of San Francisco where he would dispense 50 one hundred dollars bills to

152

the crowd. A man wearing a stocking hat recognized Fitswell and started calling out his name: "Fitswell. Fitswell. Fitswell." The crowd picked up on it, several people here and there chanting "Fitswell" with the man, until hundreds of homeless people all started to cry out in unison. "Fitswell, Fitswell–Fitswell."

Jesus Fucking Christ. I know it's a scam, Dick Fitswell muttered to himself, *but this scam--what a thing of beauty it is. At first I used the idea just so I could fuck more chicks and now it's come to this----The Dick Fitswell Homeless Fuckathon. Women, they are such idiots. I'd be taking my dates back to my apartment and ask them for donations.* "Hey baby, can I ask you for a little spare cash? Think of all the homeless who have no where to go for Christmas? I'm giving five hundred dollars of my own money to give to the homeless. Can you spare me some?" *It gets them every time. I mean how can they refuse? And if I didn't ask my dates for donations to the homeless, they'd probably think I was insensitive. Voila—I just tell them I'm giving five hundred of my own money to the homeless and they think I'm* Mr. Sensitive–the man who cares about people. *It works like a charm. Almost all of them end up fucking me and they wind up giving me their money.*

Dick Fitswell continued to roam among the homeless who littered the sidewalk, looking for the prettiest woman he could find as he thought about how he had collected six thousand from his dates while pocketing a thousand for his trouble. He first considered a brunette, who was pretty enough but not particularly striking. *She'd be okay on an off night,*" Dick Fitswell said to himself, *but tonight is Christmas Eve and I want someone I can really remember.* Then he saw her. Oozing with raw sexuality she was of a undeterminable black, Hispanic or Oriental mixture. She wore an old blue denim jacket which didn't quite hide her prominent breasts. *She's the shits,* Dick Fitswell whispered to himself. Not wasting a moment, he went right over to her.

"What are you doing on this sidewalk on Christmas Eve?" he asked her gently.

"I've been down on my luck lately. My boyfriend just kicked me out of his place."

153

"Do you have any children?"

"I have three," the woman replied. "I've been trying to get custody back but I don't have a chance until I get back on my feet again."

"I'm going to give you a place to stay tonight and two hundred dollars. That should help."

"I would love that. It's not that comfortable out on this sidewalk. Do you have anything to drink at your place?"

"Whatever you want. I have a pretty well stocked bar."

Dick Fitswell had all the essentials in his hotel room. Vodka, Gin, Beer, Wine, Bourbon, Scotch and his favorite of them all, a bottle of Tequila. He had always believed that alcohol was alcohol and that it didn't make much difference what you drank as long as it was as strong as everything else. Through years of experience he had learned that Tequila seemed to do the job much faster than practically anything else, causing most women to lose their inhibitions after only three or four shots. It didn't take long for Dick Fitswell to convince the woman to try the Tequila.

"I've found that most real men and women drink Tequila," Dick Fitswell said after they had several shots together.

"Why's that?" asked the woman.

"A real drinker wants to have that warm fiery taste going through his gullet. Or hers", Dick Fitswell added. "People who are into a feeling of heightened senses go for the Tequila. It's the real shit."

"I always wondered why I liked it," the woman replied.

"It's like flucking," said Dick Fitswell. "There's good fucking and then there's bad fucking. That's the reason I chose you. Your preference for Tequila shows that you are a woman with a heightened degree of sexual awareness. Please take your clothes off. I'll show you what I mean"

Dick Fitswell had made Egg Nog just for the occasion. He had been right about the girl. He didn't have to say another word to get her in bed. She's lucky she's got me for tonight, he said to himself. Poor thing never had a real man like me before which is why she's living out on the sidewalks of San Francisco. He crawled on top of her, pulled her legs apart with his hands, and gently started to stick his penis in her which had now swelled up to its full eighteen inches.

"God—your are tight!" he told her as he tried to wiggle it into her opening. His cock felt her lips resist his entry. But after a little thrusting he managed to get the tip of his penis into her. He felt a slight exquisite pain as she loosed up just enough for him to jam eight inches in. Pulling out of her, Dick Fitswell reached for the pitcher of egg nog and started to pour it into her opening. When he finished he lay on top of her with his penis hanging over her face and began sucking the egg nog out of her love channel.

What does this bastard think I am? thought the girl. *A dixie cup?*

Dick Fitswell didn't enjoy oral sex that much, believing it to be just the means of getting a girl to open up enough to accept his huge cock. Within five minutes he had loosened her up enough to introduce her to his full length. "Let me inject you full of Christmas spirit," he said to her as he reversed his position and plunged deep inside her. He reached under her buttocks and lifted her up against him as he started to thrust. Then he took her mouth in his, biting hard against her lips as he continued to work his ramrod deep inside her. *They like the pain*, Dick Fitswell thought, *and I am just the man to give it to them. Women love pain while they are having sex. It makes them come all over themselves.* He bit harder making sure he drew blood.

Dick Fitswell was squirting his last drops of semen into her grunting like an animal as he pulled her by the hair while still crushing his lips against hers. When he finished he lay on his back next to her and casually lit a cigarette. "Baby, when this night is over I want you to tell all your friends about me because I will return again next year and pick someone new out who's going to get lucky."

155

"Are you into bondage, Dick?"

"Not really. I like being in control and being tied up is not my idea of fun."

"Then you haven't tried it that much then. I'm really good at it. I'll make you come and come and make you my love slave."

'I don't think so. Some other night possibly."

"Are you chicken, Dick? Are you afraid of me?"

"You gotta be kidding me. There isn't a woman alive who scares me."

"Then let me tie you up. I promise you that you will remember me each Christmas for the rest of your life."

"Okay then. You have challenged me and I'm too much of a man to ever back down from a challenge," Dick Fitswell replied.

Almost five foot nine the woman was strong and athletic. Her powerful back muscles were almost imperceptible. She had a slender waist and a tight ass from all the walking she had been doing getting around in the San Francisco hills. Dick Fitswell had barely noticed the understated power in her long smooth body since becoming captivated by her beautiful breasts jutting out into her denim jacket the moment he first saw her. She had brought her back pack into his motel room from which she now retrieved two twenty foot sections of rope. Working quickly and decisively she tied his feet to the foot of the bed. Then she tied his hands and arms down to the bed frame on both sides of the mattress. She never mentioned that she loved climbing mountains and often used ropes to climb up and down cliffs.

Dick Fitswell lay in bed watching her, smugly thinking: *She tries any shit I don't like, I'm getting loose because I am Dick Fitswell and I always win.* He watched her jump off the bed onto the floor where she could put her full weight into tightening the rope imprisoning his right arm. Before it registered on Dick Fitswell that this was no game, she ran over to the left side of the bed and yanked hard against the rope. Dick Fitswell's arms felt as if they had been nearly yanked out of their sockets. She moved down to his legs and tightened the ropes that secured his feet to the foot of the bed. He felt the ropes bite deeply into his wrists.

"Your wrists will bleed a little bit," the girl told Dick Fitswell, "but that's for your pleasure, not mine. But I need to get your ass up into the air with this backpack. Positioning the backpack against him she hovered over him as she reached underneath his cheeks. Mesmerized by what she would do next, Dick Fitswell didn't resist as she slid the backpack underneath his ass which was now eighteen inches above the mattress, a distance that was ironically the length of his penis.

Dick Fitswell watched her take his penis into her mouth. He closed his eyes as she pulled the large dildo from one of the pockets of her back pack. He felt something hard being shoved up his butt hole. At first the girl moved it gently into his anus as she pushed it in and out. Not waiting for him to fully loosen up, she thrust it all the way in as soon as she got the tip of the dildo past his sphincter muscle.

"Fuck....That hurts," Dick Fitswell screamed. "You goddamn bitch. Couldn't you at least use some lubrication?"

The woman spit his cock out of her mouth as she replied, "It's Christmas Dick. I just want to give you something special."

The woman took Dick Fitswell's penis back into her mouth , sucking it as she slid the dildo back and forth. Although the pain was terrific, Dick Fitswell could still feel her moist lips all along his shaft. Now that she felt she had asserted herself the woman started to ease up on her right hand that had been thrusting the dildo up Dick Fitswell's ass. She mounted him as she gently eased the dildo back and forth, and took his huge penis deep inside her.

"Now I can talk to you, Dick. And I will keep talking to you as you come." She could feel the excitement course through Dick

Fitswell's body as he strained against the ropes, then feeling him about to come, she once again started pummeling his anal cavity with the dildo. When she felt the first globules of semen explode into her box the woman bore down on the dildo with all her strength. Dick Fitswell felt his penis exploding come between her legs as blood started to stream out of his rectum onto the sheets. He felt a brief moment of agonizing pain and blacked out.

Dick Fitswell slowly opened his eyes when he came to and saw the woman squatting over him. "Merry Christmas, Mr. Fitswell," the woman taunted. "Never forget me." She untied him only after he told her she where he had stashed his wallet and $750.00 cash under his mattress.

Dick Fitswell works for America Online

I've got the best job in the work running a server here for Assholes Online, Dick Fitswell gloated to himself. *I am regarded as a professional and one of the most intelligent men in the work force. My company is going places and it's huge. Now that I've hired Wendy, I've got a cute chick working for me. From now on I'm calling my 18 inch dick, Caesar, and my motto with these women is going to be: "I've come to bury Caesar, not to praise him." I don't care if Wendy doesn't even know how to turn a computer on so long as she keeps my cock in condition. And if she doesn't, I'm firing her tight little ass.*

Dick Fitswell had just hired Wendy for one reason only-------she was the most sensuous, gorgeous looking woman out of the five hundred women who had answered the help wanted add he had put in the paper. Blonde, and nearly five foot eight, Wendy was the embodiment of female perfection, a goddess in human form, long legged and flat bellied, who possessed the innocent blue eyed look that announced that paradox many men find so attractive, yet allusive----*I know everything about sex but I've never experienced it.*

"How about a cup of coffee, Wendy? These hours are starting to kill me." Dick Fitswell watched Wendy bend over the low table. He had purposely shortened the tables legs with a hack saw so that he could watch her trim little ass tighten each time she poured him a fresh cup and nearly creamed his pants for the fifteenth time that day. *Oh God,* Dick Fitswell thought, *I"ll bet she's so tight that I'll come and come when I get inside her. I can't wait any longer. It's time to make my move.*

"Wendy," he said as he lit a Camel, "You and I both work in a very high pressure environment for the finest and largest Internet Service provider in the World. And we are both very highly paid for what we do. America Online expects a lot from us, and we

159

cannot fail to disappoint them. The world is watching us. We must help AOL continue to dominate this industry. If we aren't ready for every eventuality, we are going to fail. And if we fail we will let America down. Our country will never forgive us. It is imperative that you and I work together as a finely tuned team, that we learn to think as one, and react as one if our computer systems ever fail."

"Our task is great, Dick. Everybody who is anybody is jumping to join cyberland with America Online," Wendy agreed.

"Wendy, sex can distract a man or a woman from work. Which is okay in most job positions but your job here with AOL is so important that you cannot let this happen to you. As your boss I feel I have to make sure it never distracts you and that your job is foremost on your mind. I want you to look upon me as the source of your every need—your need of a pay check, your need for sex, and your need for companionship so that you won't find anything wanting in this office."

"I see your point, Dick, but we just don't know each other well enough. Let's just go slow at first."

"How about a blow job then? Dick Fitswell didn't enjoy blow jobs since they passed for substitutes for the real thing causing a man to blow his wad without allowing him to achieve penetration. For Dick, achieving the perfect fit was the only thing. Blow jobs were not the means to the end. They made him lose his erection even though he got to spill his juices, which would deprive him of being able to insert his penis into that perfect love channel he had made it his quest to find. But Wendy was special and Dick Fitswell felt that having her suck his penis would make her fall in love with his irresistible appendage.

"Oh Dick, I don't know if we should. Now?"

"Now Wendy. We have to start somewhere. Take off your clothes so I can watch while you suck me. I can't feel your presence tingling my skin unless you are naked and showing off the real you."

Wendy was more than Dick Fitswell ever expected. She started to strip, then hesitated, but his eyes implored her to finish taking her clothes off, calling out to her, *Trust me. You are doing the right thing.* Her nipples hardened to his touch. When he started to stroke her between her legs, he sensed that she was his and that he would soon be inside her. Suddenly she jerked away shouting, "No. Not now. Not this time Dick. Here, just lean back while I suck your balls."

Dick Fitswell had never experienced a woman like Wendy before. Suddenly she had become assertive. It was a question of taking it or losing her. Stroking her between her thighs had almost made him come. He knew he would have ejaculated all over her stomach and licked his own come off of her just to lick her stomach. If she asked him to, he would have eaten out her asshole. For the first time in his life he felt cowed. And obeyed her, sitting back at his desk chair in front of the main computer as she leaned over his lap. He had never felt his member become so hard before as Wendy knelt over him and started to suck his balls. Suddenly Dick Fitswell felt sharp pinpoints of pain as her teeth bit into his testicles. Wendy jumped back and said: "You are mine Dick. I am going to make you come when I want you to come. Just sit back and enjoy this."

Hunching over him once more, Wendy showed off her narrow waist and trim back to Dick Fitswell as she shoved her nipples into his groin. Fitswell felt her nipples harden against his penis as she rubbed her chest across his lap. Then she inched her body backwards and took his penis into his mouth. Dick Fitswell never wanted a woman so badly in his life. He wanted his whole cock up her, then up her ass. He wanted to make her squeal. But Wendy was having none of it. Dick tried to switch positions on her. Once again she bit his testicle, then shoved him back into his chair.

"You want me Dick, don't you? You want it right up my legs but you are not going to get it until I let you and that's not going to be now. You are just going to have to come in my mouth."

Dick Fitswell once again felt his penis sliding in her wet, silky mouth. He felt her gentle sucking on his shaft and lost control as the first drops of semen started to ooze from his penis. Wendy felt his excitement surge, and tasted those first little drops before the deluge. Then she spit his penis out of her mouth. Her timing was perfect. She watched with a self satisfied smile as Dick Fitswell jettisoned come all over his computer. Some of it drenched his mouse pad--his favorite mouse pad, the one he had custom designed with an image of his own gigantic Fitswellian penis etched into its foamy surface. She was quick, jerking her body sideways so that the main force of his come spurted all over his computer. Dick Fitswell's eyes watched in disbelief as his semen squirted over the face of his computer. The problem was the computer no longer had a face since he had been using it as the main server in the office and had started putting two new hard drives into it. The computer case was lying next to his desk on the floor. Semen flooded all over the circuit boards of the exposed computer and its hard drives, Unfortunately for all the AOL members who had been dialing into the web from Fitwell's server, Dick Fitswell had spewed more come than he had ever spilled in his life. Suddenly the computer shorted out as 75000 AOL members lost their connections.

"What have we done?" asked Wendy.

"We just disconnected all our subscribers in this area. You should have let me fuck you."

"Turn on the backup systems, Dick."

"There is no backup system. AOL doesn't believe in them."

Three hours later, Dick Fitswell's supervisor, the district manager for AOL, entered Dick's office. "Well Dick, we now have 75000 customers offline. How'd you do it?" the supervisor asked.

"Come on in, Jeff. It's hard to explain but........."

The supervisor saw the main computer on Fitswell's desk, its hood off and still lying on the floor. Dick Fitswell and Wendy had

162

tried to get all the come off the desk and most of the computer but Dick knew from experience that a scrubbing of the circuit boards and some of its other parts would completely ruin it. Half congealed globules of semen still adhered to the circuitry.

"What did you two do, come all over this thing?" the supervisor asked.

"I don't want to lie to you. Yes, we did," said Fitswell. "I am really sorry. I should have used a rubber."

"Fuck it, Dick. I wouldn't worry too much about it," the supervisor replied. "You and I have been friends for a long time."

"Yeah, but we have 75000 customers offline and they aren't going to be happy campers," said Dick Fitswell.

"They are Aolers, Dick. They are used to getting a lot less and paying more for it. They are the sheep of the Internet world. They will take anything and think they are doing the right thing. That's why we call ourselves America Online.

They think that because our company name has America on it that's it's got to be a fine organization." The supervisor winked at Dick Fitswell, then smirked. "But we know better, don't we Dick? We get paid far more than we are worth and the company charges a lot more for internet access than everybody else. The hell with it. We will just have to get you new equipment and have our subscribers pay the bill.

Then the supervisor addressed Wendy. "Wendy, can I have a moment alone with Dick?"

After Wendy disappeared into the hallway outside the office, the supervisor took Dick Fitswell by the arm. "Well done Dick. I've never seen a woman so attractive. I hope you will fuck her once for me. Look, my office manager and Secretary, Holly, is getting a little old. I think she should retire. I want you to advertise for her replacement and find someone as good looking as Wendy."

Dick Fitswell works for Microcrap

"Now I've got me a real job," Dick Fitswell crowed. I'm working for the most powerful computer-communications company on earth. I've just gotta tell them who's boss and give them my terms that I'm willing to work under."

Suddenly the door to his new office opened and none other than Billy Masterbates himself walked in accompanied by Fitswell's new secretary who immediately introduced herself as Sarah Stonehenge. Dick Fitswell disliked both of them immediately, Billy Masterbates because of his condescending airs and Sarah Stonehenge because he couldn't get eye contact with her.

"Sarah Stonehenge will be working with you, Dick," said Billy Masterbates. "She is one of my most trusted employees so treat her like your shadow. Let her in on everything you do. If you do exactly what I tell you to do, your salary is going to be a million a year. All you have to do is to make most of the AOL servers work worse than they are already performing. You have all their secret passwords and user id's and the inside knowledge how to corrupt all their dialups. I will personally give you the secret Microcrap codes that's going to make all the AOL dialups run as slow as molasses.

"They are already running as slow as molasses," Dick Fitswell replied. "They can't get much worse than they already are."

"Trust me Dick. Use my Microcrap programs and they are going to do much worse. I am looking at causing them to lose half their customer base which is just what I did to Netscape."

"I have one condition for my working for you, and this is final," said Dick Fitswell. I must have my own secretary, Wendy, working for me here. I can't use Sarah."

"Why not?" Billy Masterbates asked. "I trust Sarah completely."

"Can't use her. Look at her. She's got ice running through her veins. She can't even look me in the eye. I'll bet she's never been fucked in her life and any woman I don't stand a chance of fucking I'm just not going to trust."

"Sorry Dick. I can't use you then. This is final. You either work with Sarah or you aren't going to be working for Microcrap."

"You need me and you know it, Billy. Who else has all the passwords and inside knowledge to topple AOL? I'm the only person you know who's got the knowledge and the guts to pull it off. Face it—you might not make it without me. You want world wide domination of the Internet and AOL's the only thing standing in your way. Think of the power you will have. Whole nations will be forced to knuckle under you. The information revolution will all be yours. You will have complete control of the news world wide. AOL will be History but only if you hire me."

"I hate to admit it but you are right, Dick. Okay then. From now on you report directly to me. Bring Wendy on in then. And here's the computer codes I've written up for you," Billy Masterbates replied as he handed Dick Fitswell a file folder of printouts. "Meanwhile, continue to pretend like you are working for AOL. Keep showing up for your normal job with them. You will be expected to work here only on weekends and late at night."

*****

Over at AOL Dick Fitswell had been promoted and was now working in its national headquarters thanks to his supplying most of their higher up execs with some of the best looking secretaries he could find from among the major strip clubs of the United States. On top of the building Dick Fitswell now worked in was a huge sign that could easily be seen from the interstate which read "Americans Online working together to create a better world in which you can be free." Dick Fitswell's new office consisted of four rooms. There was the main reception area in which Wendy handled the phone and greeted visitors. There was the main computer room which connected to every AOL server in the nation. Then there was Dick Fitswell's private quarters equipped with a well stocked bar, a leather chair, a roll top desk, and a huge heart shaped water bed. Adjoining it was the fourth room, a large restroom which Fitswell had designed himself. The faucets for both the lavatory and the shower were hard chrome penises which had been prepared from a mold prepared from Fitswell's very own eighteen inch penis. On each penis shaped faucet Fitswell had inscribed "Caesar".

Dick Fitswell was in the midst of celebrating with Wendy his new million dollar job with Microcrap. She sat on his waterbed as he refilled her glass with scotch from his private bar. He handed her the glass, then announced confidently: "To my new million dollar a year job and your new promotion."

"Promotion for me? What promotion?" she asked.

"You are now my right hand, not just my secretary," Dick Fitswell replied. I've always wanted to fuck you, Wendy. You are now in charge of most of my orgasms as well as your official duties to both AOL and Microcrap."

"Not on your life, Dick. I'd never lower myself to fucking someone just to keep my job."

Dick Fitswell reached into his pocket for the set of car keys and dangled them in front of her. "Look out the window, Wendy and check out that green convertible out in the parking lot." Wendy opened the drapes. Her mouth gaped open when she saw the brand new green Corvette convertible with licence plates reading "Wendy69Queen".

"That's a different story now, Dick. What do you want me to do?"

"I want you to lie on this bed on your stomach and let me give it to you up your ass. Then when we're done we are going to really get into some serious fucking."

He had wanted Wendy for months and for months she had played hard to get. Her magnificent breasts now pointed toward the covers, firm with long erect nipples. She lay face down, her head on the pillow with her back arched showing firm buttocks to the ceiling. "Time to tame the shrew," Dick Fitswell whispered quietly to himself. "She's finally mine."

"I'm going to make her pay for having me wait this long," Dick Fitswell swore under his breath as he jammed 18 inches of raging erect cock up her ass. He laughed out loud when she screamed from the pain. *I can ease it in gradually and it won't hurt as badly,* he said to himself as he grabbed her around the neck as he pumped her from behind, *but I want her to never forget this moment.* Thrusting quickly he jammed his full length into her with each thrust, coming in huge spurts while nearly strangling the breath out of her.

He let her whimper as he caught his breath lying next to her. Then he went to the bar and got each of them a shot of Cuervo. After four shots he was ready to go again. She clung tightly to him when he penetrated her with his chest pushiing up tightly against her bosom. "What do you have inside you now?" he asked her loudly.

"Your cock," she replied.

"No. That's not it. You have Caesar inside you now. Now repeat after me: "I am here not to praise Caesar but to allow him to be buried inside me."

"Very good," he told her after she repeated it. "I will ask you to repeat that each night, at least once while I am fucking you."

She was the tightest fit he had ever had. After he had come the third time Dick Fitswell announced: "I have to load some of that Microcrap code into the computer. Thank God we have that laptop networked to the main computer. It's time to put the slowdown on the AOL servers in New York City.

By this time both of them were very drunk. Dick Fitswell typed computer code into the laptop; then he ftped the new code into the AOL servers in New York City as Wendy sucked his cock clean, then brought him to his fourth orgasm with her mouth. He came the fifth time while sucking one of her succulent breasts as she straddled him.

The next night Dick Fitswell shot Microcrap code into the AOL servers in Philadelphia and Boston between injecting come into Wendy's vagina, anus and between her breasts. Two weeks later they had managed to change the code in the AOL servers on the West Coast and throughout the Midwest. Wendy and Dick Fitswell had gotten very drunk each night. By the end of the month he couldn't even think of another woman.

Dick Fitswell was fucking Wendy in his Microcrap office one Sunday afternoon when he heard the door being angrily opened. His face flushing with anger, Billy Mastergates stood before them as Wendy hurriedly put on her clothes,.

"Just what in the fuck you been doing this last month, Fitswell?"

"I've been tampering with AOL's computer code all across the U.S. just as you told me to do," Dick Fitswell replied.

"You screwed up the code, Dick. I've been having you watched. You've gotten drunk each night and you messed up that code I gave you."

"Then their servers should be doing even worse."

"But they are not Dick. Any code is better than AOL's code. You've made their servers run better than they've ever run before. The only code that could make them do worse is the exact code I supplied you with. You are fired, Dick. And take that tramp with you."

Billy Masterbates had been right. The AOL Servers had never performed better. Dick Fitswell's performance had been duly noted by the AOL higher ups. Although he had been fired from

Microcrap he should have been promoted at AOL—perhaps to the company's top position but the head man at AOL had all the evidence that had pointed to Dick Fitswell's causing AOL's improved performance destroyed, taking the credit for himself. Deciding that Dick Fitswell was a very real threat to his continued control over AOL, the head of AOL promptly fired him. Dick Fitswell found himself on the street without a job.

Pay Your Pal and the Cambodians

Disclaimer---We apologize for any confusion due to our sloppiness from using Pay Pal for Pay your Pal and vice versa.
We were drunk while editing Corbett's story and we couldn't really see any difference in Pay Pal's inability to determine between an individual's constitutional rights and Pay Your Pal's lack of respect for ancient civilizations.

Here I am. Finally, I'm set. I'm a lawyer and my future is assured, Dick Fitswell reflected as he calmly considered the last three years of his life. *I dropped out. I no longer wanted to rule an island or run a whore house or even see how many girls I could fuck. Instead I devoted myself to seven hours of study a day along with more than four hours in the classroom for three long hard years. It's about time I can devote myself to what I can do for humanity. And now, there's that appointment with those lawyers from Pay Your Pal.*

*****

But there was to be only one attorney representing Pay Your Pal in what could become the biggest supreme court case since the Dred Scott case before the Civil War. Harvey Massab lock, appeared to be the very personification of his name. His head was over a third larger than it should have been. He had heavy dark eyebrows that gave him a brooding appearance while his

170

hands appeared soft and flaccid as if he had never done an ounce of physical work in his life.

Philip Mindlessgame, the CEO of Pay Your Pal, appeared to be Harvey's opposite. Philip weighed 165 pounds, which was far too light for a man standing over six feet-six. In fact, Philip cut such a thin figure for his height that he had once been mistaken for a water reed by a massive golden retriever which had smashed right through him as the animal sprinted out into a swamp to retrieve a bird one of Philip's hunting companions had just shot. Philip was just as uncoordinated as he was too slender for his great height. When the dog knocked him down in two feet of water Philip's head had gone under. As both his head and body sunk underneath the surface at the same time, Philip had tried to raise himself from the water by his arms but found he didn't have the upper body strength to be successful. He had then tried to regain his feet by using his lower torso, but was unable to manage that too. Had he been alone he would have drowned. But one of his hunting buddies had been able to run over to him and jerk him to his feet.

Philip had swallowed nearly a cup of water which was enough to get him spitting, coughing and gurgling. And as he coughed out the stale swamp water he looked all about him through reddened eyes and swore: "I'll get you son-of a bitches for this!" he screamed. "I'll have your heads on a pike so help me God. I'll have you in court for so long, you will wish you had all been still born," he threatened while still looking around him for imaginary enemies.

But the only things he could see were the hunting companion who had just saved his life and the dog that had mistaken him for a plant. His other hunting buddies were over a hundred yards away surrounded by thick swamp brush, their visibility limited to only 25 yards.

By the time Dick Fitswell was ushered into the executive conference room at the Pay Your Pal Needle Dome, Philip Mindlessgame had cooled down, but just a little.

"I'm not in a very good mood right now, so let me cut this one to the quick," said Philip. "It's those fucking Cambodians. They have violated our service agreement when they started using Fuk Sam Bay to buy all those used tires from the Cubans. So we are bringing them to court here in the U.S. With any kind of luck we can freeze all their assets that are being held by the Bank of America."

"And I am the attorney representing the Cambodians," Dick Fitswell replied. "Now could you please tell me how they have violated Pay Your Pal's users' agreement."

"Well it's pretty fucking obvious, isn't it. It's their goddamn temples at Angkor Vat. They have pornography all over those walls. Sickening shit, it really is. Those fuckers have no culture and no class. For years those pricks over there in Cambodia have been poisoning the minds of American tourists with all those naked breasts in all those Angkor Wat temple walls."

"But I'm not so sure the Cambodians have enough assets in American banks worth going after," said Harvey Massablock.

"I don't really give a shit," said Philip. "It's the goddamn principal that counts. Obscenity must be punished wherever we fucking find it."

"Who says these naked breasts are obscene? I want to know who has the right to declare them obscene . The Buddhists have had them on those temples over in Angkor Vat for over eight hundred years. And not only that, they have them in similar structures in Laos, Thailand, and Vietnam. And there's similar places in China not to mention in Yucatan and over a dozen similar places in the world, all of which represents great civilizations of the past," Dick Fitswell pointed out.

"They are nude statues. Pal Your Pal says they are obscene," said Philip. "And they are a fucking goddamn insult to all decent God fearing Christians throughout the entire world."

"Ever think those Buddhists can give a rat's ass about the Pay Your Pal user's agreement?" said Dick Fitswell. I also want to mention that the way Pay Your Pal has been trying to enforce its user's agreement is in direct violation of the 1st Amendment of the U.S. Constitution that provides all Americans with freedom of speech, freedom of the press, and freedom of expression."

"Fuck the U.S. Constitution," Philip shouted. "That piece of shit is outmoded. The U.S. Constitution might have been okay back in 1800 but people are different today with different needs. We at Pay Your Pal are meeting those needs that are not being met for the modern day man and woman. And one of the things sorely lacking today is the fucking lack of values and of good taste."

"And you think the Cambodians are lacking in good tastes?" asked Dick Fitswell.

"Goddamn right they are! Why they got those naked breasts implanted all over their temples, those motherfuckers!"

"Have it your way, Philip, Harvey Massablock replied. "But Dick Fitswell does have a point. "I really don't think we can win this in court. Well, we might at first, but by the time it hits the Supreme Court, any decision in your favor is likely to be reversed."

"Well then, we will just have to have one or two of those Supreme Court justices assassinated, won't we? I'll get in touch with some of my underworld connections right away. It's about time that decency is restored back in this great country of ours," said Philip.

"Do you think it's wise that you say things like that in front of Dick, here? Harvey asked.

"I don't think Dick is in much of a position to do anything about it," said Philip. "We got him on video tape doing all kinds of nasty shit to more girls than most of us would dream of fucking in a lifetime. I got enough fucking shit on Dick to get him disbarred from the legal profession and probably enough to get him some jail time for what he's done to underage girls."

Dick Fitswell was speechless, perhaps for the first time in his life. He remembered having sex with girls under 18 on a few occasions. But there were also those many times he didn't remember or didn't care what age the girls were. He also knew there were government entities that did not shirk from gathering incriminating evidence against many Americans, especially those who operate on a high profile. He also knew that it wouldn't take much for a company with Pay Your Pal's resources to either buy such videos or to get their own made in house.

"But I think we need a more permanent solution," Philip added. "We are going to have to bomb all those temples into oblivion in order to make the world safe for American ideals. I think a half a billion dollars should do it. There are several very violent groups operating in Cambodia today that will do exactly what I ask them to do if we give them enough money. The North Koreans are perfectly willing to provide me with a tactical nuclear bomb for the right money. And they will ship anywhere I want the package delivered. Pay Your Pal will have a package delivered to Angkor Vat that will be marked "raw materials" which everybody's going to think consists of lumber and tools to be used for temple repair. In fact, what I am having delivered is much more than a tactical nuclear weapon. It's the real thing. Nothing diminished in size with this thing. It will be enough to completely level every temple in Angkor Vat. Everything within miles in fact ."

"But don't you think this is going a little too far?" Harvey Massblock asked in complete disbelief.

"Not at all. I fully intend on making the entire world safe for all of us Christians. It will be a far more fucking safe place to live in and for the first time Christian morals and values will be made a matter of primal concern for everybody.?"

Two weeks later a nuclear bomb went off in Cambodia completely leveling Angkor Vat. Those responsible were presumed dead along with thousands of others that included a large number of tourists from a number of different nations as well as Cambodian citizens living close by. To a small group of confidants, Philip would later boast that he had "those Cambodian breasts"

174

surgically removed. Both the American government and media blamed it all on suicide bombers representing a terrorist group of unknown origin. Except for the Cambodians, the world hardly noticed since it had been getting used to the idea of massive terrorist attacks using weapons of mass destruction for some time. Throughout the U.S. security measures were tightened everywhere with new systems being purchased for billions of dollars. By this time Pay Your Pal had invested large sums of money in those companies manufacturing the security systems that landed the most government contracts. Meanwhile, perhaps for the first time in his life, Dick Fitswell felt completely powerless at his inability to do something that he felt was truly important.

Dick Fitswell moves back to Thailand

Unable to stop Pay Your Pal from bombing Angkor Wat into oblivion, for the first time in his life, Dick Fitswell was filled with despair. Pay Your Pal had joined forces with the Mothers for a More Boring Nation after finding out the temples of Angkor Wat were openly displaying women's tits on many of its sculptures. What had especially galled the powers that be at Pay Your Pal was not the actual display of tits. It was the fact that these sculptures were hundreds of years old, and that they portrayed actual dancing girls who had publicly displayed their breasts in what must have been ancient strip clubs. Those Mothers for a More Boring Nation who had formed the top executive ranks at Pay Your Pal believed that all strip clubs were a malignant cancer undermining the morality of Christian America.

Central to the Mothers for a More Boring Nation's core philosophy was that strip clubs represented something new that was unique to the twentieth century and that they had been created by demonic creatures who had surfaced as strip club owners. The top executives at Pay Your Pal had been shocked to find that the sculptures and frescos depicting topless strippers in Cambodia actually existed and that new evidence was being discovered by archeologists in Tikal, Guatemala, Africa, and even Thailand; that something very similar to strip clubs had existed for centuries, perhaps even thousands of years.

It followed that strip clubs had been universally accepted all over the planet. These discoveries conflicted with the ninth commandment of the Mothers for a More Boring Nation's handbook--"Thou shall not go to strip clubs" and the tenth commandment proscribing that "these nests of evil must be closed down" because public nudity was evil.

Dick Fitswell had long ago decided it was the other way around. Pure logic dictated that absolute condemnation of public nudity

176

made no sense at all since obviously a bare ass that had never been exposed to the sun was a very ugly thing indeed especially when the rest of the body was well tanned thus exposing the sickly whiteness of what swimming suits and bikinis covered up. Dick Fitswell had decided that nothing less than the complete devotion of his life to combating the Mothers for a More Boring Nation would be worthy of such a talented man as himself. He decided to take a year's sabbatical off from his law office to spend it in Thailand where he could find the most effective means of fighting the Mothers for a More Boring Nation.

Dick Fitswell had learned while running a Bangkok whore house that Bangkok didn't hold a candle to Pattaya when it came to unbridled sexual license. Whereas Bangkok was a huge city that had just three main centers of depravity—Pat Pong, Soi Cowboy, and Nana Plaza, much of Pattaya was a single contigous zone of bars, massage parlours and night clubs that extending for miles. Walking Street alone had over 50 strip clubs. On top of that there were over 2000 beer bars scattered throughout the city with each one having anywhere from three to fifteen "hostesses" whose main goal was to go back to a customer's room to fuck his brains out. Fitswell had sampled all of Walking Street's go go bars, and although he liked what they had to offer–which was plenty of sex, he had found them not quite up to what he had in mind.

"Which was what?" Fitswell couldn't even answer his own question. "Exactly what is it that I'm looking for?" He decided to take a long walk. He started near Big C on Second Road on Soi 2 and slowly made his way down to Soi Seven. He then walked all the way down Soi 7 to Beach Road passing over a hundred bars and at least five hundred whores working them, some of them calling out to him, "Hey sexy man." Two or three bar girls came out into the middle of Soi Seven where they took him by hand trying to coax him into accompanying them into their bars to buy them drinks. Not finding anything that was too delectable to pass up, he walked one block South on Beach Road to Soi 8 and proceeded to take it all the way back to 2nd Road.

Soi 8 was just like Soi 7 except Dick Fitswell thought the girls were even friendlier and better looking. Most but not all the bars were lined up in bar complexes that opened out onto the street. These were twenty feet wide at the most. Consisting of two rows of bar stools that faced each other the bar girls stood inside these two rows servicing their customers across cheap counter tops. Each bar had a mama san or "big boss" and a cashier keeping track of the money. Each bar had six to ten bar girls functioning as bartenders. These bar girls would take each customer's drink order, bring him his drink, and then put a little container in front of him with his bill inside . Customers rarely paid in advance since it was common practice for the bar girls to keep track of his bin which he would then settle with the bar before leaving. The girls also had games behind the bar: dice, dominoes, and Connect Four which was a three dimensional version of Tic Tak Toe which had forty-two squares one placed his counters. A player won when he was able to place four of his counters in a row. The whole idea was to get the customer and a bar girl together in a situation where there would be no language barrier. Also–once a customer started playing these games with one of the bar girls it would be very awkward of him to refuse to buy her a drink. The girls were much more than bartenders however. Each girl could be taken out of the bar for a bar fine of 200-300 baht (six to nine dollars). Above and beyond the bar fine the customer would then be expected to pay the girl a tip for her sexual services that would typically run 500 to 1000 baht for a short time which was anything short of spending the whole night with the customer and 1000 baht for long time.

A young girl sidled up to Fitswell just half way up the Soi and whispered in his ear. "Buy me drink in bar Sexy man." One look at her trim little waist, long legs, and prominent pointy breasts trying to jump out of her t-shirt invited him to say yes. He felt an immediate warmth in his groin as her breasts beckoned at him. Her slender body had him already imagining himself stabbing his big penis up between her gorgeous legs shooting semen up into her as she screamed at him to stop.

He followed her to her bar and took a bar stool up beside her. Then she asked him what he wanted to drink and when he replied—"a Heineken", she asked him if he'd buy her a shot of tequila.

After she drank her second tequila, she said, "Feel my milk."

Dick Fitswell slipped his hand up her t-shirt and found firm her breasts that were even larger than he expected. As he pulled at her nipples, the girl leaned into him then for a second pulled away, looking at him intently. She closed her lips over his and stuck her tongue into his mouth as he felt her hand close on his crouch, her finger tips flowing across his penis, before then a firm squeeze across the middle of his dick nearly jolted him from his bar stool. She was still squeezing when he felt her other hand massaging his balls. He wanted her–God, he wanted her.

But then he thought back to the vow that he had made to himself before setting out on his walk. First he had promised himself not to have more than two beers. The second thing he had promised himself was not to bar fine anyone–no matter how attractive the girl might be. He gently reached down and grasped both of her arms, just hard enough to lift them away from his crotch. He blurted out to her. "No. Not now. I cannot."

"She shot back at him, "No. You no want?"

"Yes. I want you very much. Pomme chop kun mach mach." Then he pointed at his watch and added. "Song tum" which meant eight o'clock. "I must go bye bye."

But before he check binned and left the bar he got her phone number after giving her his number and tipped her a hundred baht.

He walked all the way to Walking Street, non stop, without going into any bars, then he turned around and headed back to his hotel. Then he saw her. She was sitting alone underneath a palm tree scrutinizing him before he got even several hundred meters past Walking Street. Considering that most of the free lancers plying their trade along Pattaya's Beach are girls who can't or aren't willing to get a job in the bars or go-go's and their low ball

179

short time price of just five hundred baht for a short time, most of the street walkers aren't very attractive. But there's hundreds to choose from along the mile long palm tree lined stretch from Walking Street to Soi Six. The girl watching him was the best looking free lancer he had seen for a long time.

"Hello. How are you?" the girl asked him in clear distinct English.

"I'm going home now. Just taking a walk." Dick Fitswell replied.

"And where are you staying?" the girl asked.

"Not far. I'm staying at the Tropicana Hotel."

"Why are you alone?"

"Because I want to be alone. I'm just taking a walk and thinking."

"Are you sure you want to be alone?"

Dick Fitswell was surprised at the girl's curiosity and her excellent command of the English language. This combined with her good looks caused him to reconsider exactly what he was doing out walking alone on a beach trying to get away from it all.

"I'm not sure," Dick Fitswell replied.

"Would you like some company?" the girl asked him as she looked him intently in the eye.

"Would you go with me short time for 500 baht?"

"Sure. I can go with you now," the girl replied as she rose from the concrete bench she had been sitting on.

She walked alongside him down one of the many sois connecting Beach Road to 2nd Road–a distance of one long city block. Beach Road and Walking Street run parallel to each other as both streets are one ways with the traffic down Beach Road going to Walking Street. Dick Fitswell flagged down a baht taxi going

180

down 2nd road towards his hotel. A converted small Japanese pick up truck, the baht taxi had a special heavy bracket mounted where the bumper normally went. This bracket had a wide step for passengers to step onto while entering the pickup bed from the rear. This bracket also functioned to anchor the rear side of the canopy extending above the pickup bed to keep rain off the passengers seated there. Two narrow bench seats had been bolted into the pickup's bed so that up to twelve passengers could sit on them facing each other. On the metal braces that formed the skeleton for the canopy there were several electronic switches that were no more than door bells that had been specially designed for that peculiar Thai contrivance called a Song Taow that was often called the baht taxi. Hundreds of Song Taows serviced the Pattaya area with a large percentage of them patrolling all the way up and down Beach Road and Second Road in search of passengers who normally paid just 10 baht to ride to whatever spot they wanted to go to as long as it was on the Song Taow's normal route. One normally didn't have to wait for more than two minutes standing along either Second or Beach Road without having at least one baht taxi come along. Although the normal fare was just 10 baht (around 30 cents) while using the Song Taow as a bus a passenger might also use it as a cheap short distance taxi to go anywhere he liked in the Pattaya area so long as he negotiated a fee that was agreeable to the driver—a fee that usually could go anywhere from 100 to 200 baht. The baht bus driver (who was usually its owner as well) would then deviate from his normal route to drive his new passenger to whatever destination had been agreed upon.

Dick Fitswell only had to wait thirty seconds for the first baht taxi to pull up alongside him. The girl followed him up the low step where the bumper would have been. Then she sat close to him holding his hand as they rode up Second Road to his hotel where he rang one of the electric buzzers signaling the driver to pull to pull over. Fitswell was the first to get out of the taxi so that he could quickly walk around the Song Taow to pay the driver a twenty baht note. The driver nodded solemnly and drove back into the traffic as Fitswell took the girl into his hotel.

Sometimes a hotel will charge a guest or joiner's fee whenever a man takes a prostitute back to his room. His hotel didn't. Fitswell did notice that as he took the girl over to the elevator the night girl standing behind the reception desk looked at him a little oddly, then smiled as if she was harboring some deep dark secret known only to herself.

In his room he asked the girl if she'd rather have a Bacardi Breezer or a bottle of Singha beer and was surprised when she chose the beer. He also noticed that she never filled the glass he had offered her from the bottle. Instead she drank from the bottle just as a man would. For the first time since coming to Pattaya the thought of actually fucking a girl he had just taken back to his room never crossed his mind. A good twenty minutes had gone by as the pair drank beer together and Fitswell answered whatever questions the girl asked him.

"What country do you come from?" the girl asked him.

Fitswell was surprised to hear the girl ask him the question that particular way. Nearly every Thai whore will ask, "Where do you come from?" as one of several standard questions nearly all of them ask. He had learned that where he came from really didn't matter because over ninety percent of the Thai girls wouldn't be able to come within four thousand miles of placing it on a map anyway. He noticed how this particular girl had phrased the question—"What country" which was a much more precise way of asking him what most girls didn't give a rats ass about in the first place.

"The United States," he replied.

"How expensive is a hotel room like this one?" she asked in perfect English.

"I'd say about eighty American dollars. I'm paying just thirty dollars for this one so it will cost about two and a half times more."

"What do you like about Thailand?" she then asked.

The first beer soon became the second beer. The girl was in no hurry to get on with the short time seeming to be genuinely interested in him. Finally he decided to break off all conversation and to get on with what he had brought her back to his room for in the first place. "Come to my shower with me right now," he told her.

"I will be happy to," she replied as she got up from the couch the two had been sitting on and laid her second bottle of beer on the little table next to it. "You don't mind if I go in the shower with you and wash you?" she asked him.

In the shower he noticed that she faced slightly away from him, sideways–which gave him a good view of her profile. She was only average height for a Thai girl which was possibly five foot two. Her breasts were medium size with prominent dark nipples. Her waist although trim was not quite as narrow as he expected. But her belly was nice and flat. He expected all of his women to have lean flat bellies feeling that any girl with a gut either overindulged herself from overeating or had been created from inferior genes. Long ago Fitswell had expected only the best–except for those times he had gotten drunk. But he was a long way from being drunk now. He had been perfectly sober by the time he finally met the girl on the beach and he had only been on his second beer before taking her into the shower with him.

"Here, let me wash you," the girl told him in a low melodic voice.

She sidled up behind him. Unable to see her, he felt both of her hands rubbing soap all along his shaft handling him expertly. Then he felt her hands move down to the bottom of his balls. This time he felt something being plastered across his balls that didn't feel quite like soap. It felt more like Vaseline, and the girl was using plenty of it as she continued to rub it into his scrotum. He her head moving between his legs and two lips sucking up his balls. The girl continued to suck his balls softly and then she moved onto his penis which had now expanded to its full 18 inch length.

"Oh my God," he heard her exclaim. "You are very very big."

"Do you think you can get the whole thing in your mouth?" he asked.

"I cannot. But how does this feel?

Surprisingly she got a full nine inches into her mouth which she started to suck in and out but she could still get only half of it in. Spitting it out, she took its whole length into one of her hands and started to lick it from the tip all the way to where it disappeared into his scrotal sack. Never in his entire life had Little Fitswell felt so good. Although he had hundreds of women in his non-ending quest for the perfect fit, Dick Fitswell had never encountered anyone who could give him a blow job this good.

Fitswell moved his legs around her so that she could no longer suck on his dick and reached down and grabbed her around her waist. He picked her clear off her knees and placed her so that she faced away from him in a standing position. Her nice trim little ass was tightly muscled with just the right amount of curve to it. He liked his women to have firm muscular bodies with the key descriptive word to be firm rather than muscular. He had found that most women never bothered to exercise which left them with a spongy feel to them. He could best compare them to having to eat Kentucky Fried chicken, being fully aware that the chickens had been raised in confinement pens practically on top of each other where they could barely move while being almost force fed a diet that would ensure the maximum gain in weight in the shortest period of time. It was all about money, he had long ago decided and had nothing to do with taste with each chicken farmer trying to get the maximum weight gain per day. And in the case of KFC had been able to cover up the resulting low quality of taste by a lot of salt and other spices.

By this time of his life, Fitswell had fucked so many women that he had developed an acute of taste when it came to cunnilingus. Fat women had a certain sweet taste about them which he had found to be utterly horrible that can best be described as meat that had been left to rot whereas girls that even he considered to be far too skinny oftentimes gave off a rancid odor. Fitswell wasn't sure why this happened. The best answer he could give was that their metabolisms had gone into hyper mode which had caused them to become too skinny in the first place and that it was this hyperactivity of bodily functions that caused them to smell so bad.

He knew from experience that this girl would have a terrific taste to her. Fitswell pressed his large appendage firmly up against her well formed buttocks. He heard her call out, "Oh my God. You turn me on!"

He decided not to wait to get her into his bedroom. "I will bang her right now!" he said aloud. Then he pulled away from her and pressed his fingers between her legs knowing that she'd lubricate right up and that he'd be inside of her within thirty seconds.

"Do it. Give it to me," she screamed. "I want your cock inside me!"

Reaching inside her legs his fingers found her clitoris. It was large and firm. "Too large: what in the hell is this?" Fitswell cried out.

He felt the clitoris start to grow between his fingers until it expanded to three inches. "This is not right," Fitswell thought almost aloud. "It's like a dick. But it's much smaller than a dick."

Then it dawned on him. What he was about to fuck wasn't a girl. It was a man with the dick the size of a twelve year old boy's who had not reached his full maturity yet. His penis was fully erect within a few seconds of coming. Had he thrust himself deep inside her in the rear entry position Dick Fitswell knew he couldn't restrain himself for more than a few seconds. A liquid warmness had enveloped his privates. But although he knew he could not stop the sudden volcano from erupting inside his groin, he also knew that he would recuperate within fifteen minutes and that would allow him to bang the girl a second and even a possible third time.

The girl, guy, it, suddenly realized Fitswell had just discovered she wasn't exactly what she had seemed to be. Acting quickly she grabbed Fitswell's dick and started jerking him off with rapid short strokes of her hand.

Fitswell still had not recovered from his shock from finding out he was about to fuck a man when he felt his close to exploding cock continue on at full erection just seconds away from exploding hot semen all over the shower. He reached down, grabbing the kathoey's wrist, which forced the kathoey to grimace for a moment in pain as he relinquished his hold on Fitswell's penis. Fitswell did this instinctively, not because he was suddenly turned off but because in spite of just finding out his sex partner was not what he had bargained for, he was still about to come and he wanted to prolong the magic moment.

"Why you want me to stop?" the katoey suddenly asked.

"We talk now. Go in the bedroom with me now," Fitswell commanded.

The katoey followed Fitswell into the bedroom, lay down on his back with his head on the pillow, and watched Fitswell intently, his eyes gazing directly into Fitswell's. Fitswell went back into his living room for the two unfinished beers, then he went back into the bedroom, handed the katoey his unfinished beer, and sat next to him.

"You not know I am katoey?" the girl asked.

"No. Not until now," Fitswell replied.

"I am same same lady," the katoey added. Only no pussy. But I have silicon." He, she pointed at her breasts, now fully erect.

"I don't know what to say. I never fucked a man before."

"But I am not a man. I am woman."

"Then why do you have a dick?" Fitswell asked.

"Because there was mistake. But only mitnoi (a little mistake)."

"I never fuck men, and I never will," Fitswell said.

"But you feel good. I know. I see your banana and you are about to come. I know you like it."

Fitswell thought about what the katoey had just said, and decided that he could not disagree. The truth was he had been turned on more than he had remembered getting turned on for years. He started to reconsider his position. He could kick the katoey out of his room and never see her again. He could even give her a tip, possibly even pay the katoey the full five hundred baht. It was only fifteen dollars in the first place. But then he'd never know. The katoey had brought him to the very verge of erupting. So what was the harm in that? Suppose the katoey had gotten him off in his mouth, swallowed his cum, and then put his clothes back on without Fitswell ever discovering that he had a penis. He would have remembered this night as being one of his most memorable ever.

"You like me?" the katoey asked.

"Yeah, I like you." Fitswell had to admit that the katoey was more likeable than any Thai girl he had ever met. The language barrier had always stopped him from ever feeling close to a Thai woman, but it was more than that. He could always tell that no matter what they said about his being a sexy man, or liking his big dick, or their liking American men more than any other men, that it was all bull shit. It was all part of the game which was to separate him from his money. With the katoey he had felt a genuine sincerity. Even more important–the katoey's intelligence was beyond question. He or she had asked him a lot of intelligent questions and in nearly perfect English no less.

Fitswell crept up to the katoey so that he was almost on top of the person lying flat on her back in his bed. She did not look like a man. She didn't even talk like a man. She didn't have an adams apple, and she had very nice firm breasts–a woman's breasts, not a man's. He still could not get it into his head that he was talking to a man. Only his intellect told him otherwise. Still he could not fathom it. But the real bottom line was-his dick was still hard. Fitswell pried the katoey's legs apart so that he could get a good look at his credentials.

It was only a small dick. Fitswell had never been this close to a dick before, but it was getting really weird. It wasn't really a dick. He tried to imagine what an overgrown clitoris might look like. *Certainly it might be possible for a clitoris to reach a full three inches long. The clitoris might belong to a freakish occurrence-a one in a million type of girl but she would be a girl all the way. Supposing, she had a perfect body other than having an overly large clitoris, perfect breasts, wondrously long legs, a perfect ass and looks to kill. Would he bang her?* The question didn't even deserve an answer. Of course he would. He'd be an idiot not to.

Then why not fuck the katoey? What was really the difference? The only thing that separated the katoey from being a beautiful woman was the katoey had an overly large clitoris-or dick. What the hell. What's really the difference? Fitswell finally decided.

Fitswell started playing with the katoey's dick. It didn't feel like he would have expected a dick to feel, Fitswell suddenly concluded. "And if I don't have sex with this katoey now I'll go through the entire rest of my life not knowing what it's really like."

He lay down on his back next to the katoey, still completely naked, his penis sticking right up at the ceiling. The katoey changed positions moving to the lower part of the bed on her stomach so that she now faced Fitswell's lower extremities. Fitswell felt gentle hands sliding up and down his still oily shaft bringing it to the fullest erection that he had felt for years. Then he felt more of the Vaseline like substance being rubbed into his entire private area.

"My name is Gemini," the katoey suddenly announced. What I am now doing is putting something on your banana that is going to make it taste like fruit. It is going to taste real good, like melon."

Gemini continued to fondle Fitswell's penis and balls with the most exquisite touch Fitswell ever remembered feeling. And then she started to smoke him in her mouth. Fitswell completely relaxed, enjoying every moment, completely resigned to the fact that he was finally going through with it, finally determined to enjoy every sensation to the fullest.

Fitswell grasped her in his arms and pulled her over on top of his chest. Then he position her so that her penis was right up against his mouth. Firm beautiful buttocks hovered just over him as she continued to suck his cock while rubbing his oily balls between her fingertips. For the first and only time in his life, Fitswell leaned up and took a penis firmly into his mouth. He started to suck it back and forth as he arched the lower half of his body deep into the katoey's face.

It took just thirty seconds for Fitswell to come into Gemini's mouth. He exploded once, twice, three times until the explosions got weaker and weaker and he continued to explode until he felt he had finally finished yet he still felt some of his semen oozing out of his penis as Gemini sucked it all down her throat. Fitswell continued to suck on Gemini's penis which never seemed to get any larger than three inches. Finally, after a full fifteen minutes Gemini's penis seemed to grow, finally reaching a maximum length of four inches. And then Fitswell felt the katoey's semen spurting into his mouth.

Fitswell had a third beer with Gemini before escorting her to the elevator of his hotel. He didn't feel a single trace of remorse. "It is funny how this happens to most guys who've stayed in Thailand a little too long," Gemini told him. Fitswell agreed with her. He had seen time and time again how long held values and prejudices seem to go by the way side once a man actually moved to Pattaya. Just before Fitswell gave her the 500 baht he had promised Gemini told him, "you just come see me where I work when I'm not on the beach."

"Where is that?" Fitswell asked.

"On Soi Six. At the Pat Bar. Come see me."

"Do you think I will like it there?" Dick Fitswell asked.

"I think you will love Soi Six," Gemini replied. "It is everything you have ever dreamed about. It is you, Dick. I think I know you by now and I think you will be spending a lot of your time over at Soi Six."

"Where is it?"

"It is only two blocks from this hotel. When you leave your hotel, just walk towards Big C. It's only two minutes. My bar is near Beach Road."

After escorting Gemini to the elevator, Fitswell went back into his suite where he drank his third and then his fourth beer alone. He calmly concluded: *I knew something would happen to me that would be very important. Tomorrow I will go to Soi Six and see why Gemini thinks I will like it so much. Perhaps Gemini is to be my guiding light to finding out what it is that's so important for me to do.*

Soi Six

There are over 60 bars on Soi Six, the most infamous street of them all in a city that has so many bars, massage parlors, and go-go's that it's impossible to count them all. Each day the number changes as new bars appear while older ones go out of business, but it is generally agreed the number is up in the thousands. What makes Soi Six different is that nearly all its bars are air conditioned, and that means one has to physically open a closed door to gain admittance, unlike the open air beer bars where nearly everything is visible. Which is a very critical difference to the expat who has a steady Thai girlfriend because once he's inside a Soi Six Bar he can do whatever he likes with little fear of being seen by anyone outside the bar. Dick Fitswell nearly tripped on a drunken Englishman who sat scrunched up on the floor just outside the toilet getting a blow job from one of the bar girls. Already on his third beer waiting for Gemini, Dick had been watching another customer sitting in a lounge chair licking a girl's privates who was facing him while a second girl gave him head while kneeling between his legs. When Dick returned to his barstool after relieving himself, he found Gemini waiting for him.

"Gemini, do you really like this bar?" Dick asked the ladyboy.

"I like it very much," Gemini replied. "Do you like it?"

"No I don't. The place has no class."

"What do you mean?"

"See that man nearly passed out in front of the toilet getting a blow job?"

"I see him. What's the problem?"

"Do you see the other customer with those two ladies over on that chair?"

"Yes. But that's normal."

"That's normal getting blow jobs in front of everyone?" Dick asked increduously.

"Yes. It's perfectly normal on Soi Six."

*****

After making a few trips to Soi Six Dick Fitswell had started to realize the true beauty of the street. Angry Pussy sat next to him in the King Kong Bar while Dick extolled the many virtues of Soi Six to the German sitting on his left.

"Notice how I'm sitting here talking to you normally, and Angry Pussy is sitting on the other side of me massaging my dick as if it's the most normal thing to do in the world," Dick said to the German.

"Yah. This is a great place," the German replied. "Much better than Walking Street which is only for tourists and other stupid people."

"That's right. I haven't even bought Angry Pussy a drink yet and here she is trying to keep me happy. Even if I don't buy her a drink, she will probably keep rubbing my cock for the next half hour. But I'm going to buy her at least one drink anyway, and then I think I'm going to bang her."

"This lady. Why do you call her Angry Pussy?"

"She's beautiful, don't you think so?" Dick asked the German.

"Yes. She is very striking."

"The reason I call her Angry Pussy is she's as beautiful with her clothes off as she is with them on. She has wonderful nipples and she doesn't have an ounce of fat on her. She's slender in the waist and she's actually quite tall for a Thai girl. Has terrific legs too, but she doen't shave her privates."

192

"So does she have a big bush?" the German asked.

"No, she doesn't, and that's why I call her Angry Pussy. Everything about her, from her hair to her smile and her body itself is so nice and soft. She's utterly perfect in every way and then when you see her naked she has this coarse pubic hair that sticks out as if each hair is on little springs."

"She is beautiful. She's a very beautiful girl," said the German.

"That's just it," said Dick. "You go down to Walking Street now, and many of the girls are asking 2000 baht just for a short time. That's nearly "sixty-five bucks U.S. and the barfine is now at least 600 baht and it's oftentimes as much as 700 or 800 baht which means just to get a girl out of the bar a man has to shell out twenty to twenty-five dollars."

"That's completely crazy," said the German, and it's one of many reasons I never go to Walking Street anymore."

Not to mention if you have a Thai girlfriend what are you going to do in a Walking Street go-go? If you barfine a girl out of the go-go and anyone who knows your girlfriend sees you walking around with another woman, she's going to be calling your girlfriend on her cell phone within fifteen minutes, whereas here guys can be getting a blow job in front of the whole bar and the only people who are going to know about it are the handful of people who are actually in the bar. A man's Thai girlfriends are not going to be going into these places so no one's the wiser."

"I pay just 500 baht to get laid," said the German. And the rooms upstairs here are only 300 baht so my total cost is just 800 baht which is $24.00."

"Well....that does it, talking to you and seeing how much we agree on everything has now made me decide to go ahead and do it."

"And what's that?"

"I'm going to wind up buying this place."

"What? The King Kong Bar?"

"Yes. But I am going to change its name to Big Dicks."

Big Dicks

True to his word, Dick Fitswell bought the bar, which isn't exactly the truth because non-Thais are not allowed to buy houses, bars or any other real estate in Thailand with condos being the only exception. So he had managed to get a five year lease on the place. Outside hanging over his entryway, Fitswell had a huge neon sign that read, "Big Dick's." Beneath it was a smaller sign that read, "All customers must do what the Angry Pussy says."

It was all a clever bit of marketing on Dick's part. Other Soi Six Bars had clever names such as BJ's, Short Time Express, the Lick Bar, Hole in One, Quicky Bar, the Butterfly Bar, and La La land which got the point across that they were oasises of Hedonism, but Fitswell took such merchandising one step further. For one thing he had carefully trained Angry Pussy to act the part of her name on the assumption that a lot of men fantasize about being abused by beautiful women. Dick made Angry Pussy his bartender while instructing her to be a real smart ass to most of the bar's new customers. Oftentimes she'd say such things as "What are you here for, getting your dick wet like all the others?" to a new customer. Or she might come out with something really off the wall such as, "You look like you have a really small dick. Want me to get one of my girls to come over and stretch it?"

This last line fit in really well with Big Dick's best known feature which was the long display of various objects and jars behind the bar. The jars contained various creatures such as Cobras and Sea Snakes, Sea Horses and bulls' testicles fermenting in strong rice wine. So when new customers came in who appeared to be interested in the objects on display, Dick would often try to cajole them into downing shots containing the liquid contents of one of the jars.

But the star attraction of Big Dicks was the display of penis sculptures Dick kept next to the jars of sea creatures and other wine soaked horrors. The bar had obained the casts from men who had volunteered to have plaster casts made of their penises for display with each member's name and penis size appearing below them.

To be eligible for such membership a man had to submit a five hundred baht fee, evuivalent to $15.00. Then he had to chug a shot of rice wine laden with essence of snake, seahorse or bull's testicle. Finally, he had to submit to having his penis and balls encased in plaster to have a mold taken to be admired and extolled by future generations of customers.

Fitswell went over to the German sitting by himself at the bar. It was the same German who had inspired him to startup up his own bar. "Well how do you like my new place now that we have your balls and penis on display for everyone to see?" Fitswell asked the German.

"I think you are going to see me here at your bar at least three times every week," the man replied.

"Be honest, Gunther, how do you really feel about having your nine inch dick out in the open where everyone can see it in the form of that cast?"

"It makes me feel really good, Dick. It makes me feel as if I'm part of something that is much bigger than myself. It makes me feel as if I'm part of an elite fraternity representing some of the finest men in Pattaya."

Gunther's reply brought Angry Pussy to the verge of laughter as she stook behind the bar listening. But she was able to keep her composure, but only for a period of a few seconds before she could bolt for the toilet, which allowed her some semblance of privacy as she burst out laughing in front of one of the mirrors.

"Go on," Fitswell continued to urge the German. Please tell me more. Was it a good marketing gimmick on my part or was it a stupid idea?"

"I think it was a terrific idea, Dick. Here I've got my dick right out there in the open. And although 9 inches is quite large, it's not nearly as large as your 18 inch dong. But you are a living legend so you really don't count. Mine is still one of the largest behind your bar so that makes me bigger than practically anyone else and therefore more of a man. And most guys who have submitted their penises feel that they have done something that most men would never have the guts to do so they now feel braver and stronger than most men and that keeps them coming back to your bar where they feel they can find others similar to themselves.

There would be no blow jobs just outside the toilet. Moreover Angry Pussy never let anyone have sex on one of the couches or for that matter anywhere in the bar except for upstairs. Girls were allowed to grab men by their dicks and to give dick massages while sitting with them at the bar but that was about it. Dick had even bought Angry Pussy a small leather black jack which he had instructed her how to use by sharply cracking a customer across his balls for such improprieties as pulling his dick out.

My place ozzes with class, Dick Fitswell reflected to himself. *My short time rooms upstairs don't have cheap beds in them like most of the other places on this street. I've spent a great deal of money on each one having had their bedframes and headboards custom designed and hand made up in Chiang Mai in the shape of penises. This is what I was born to do so I think I'm going to stick around in Pattaya for a long time.*

One week later

Dick Fitswell was on his sixth beer drinking with Gemini in an outdoor beer bar on Soi 8 when the beggar rolled up to them on his skateboard. Although Dick's sexual encounter with the ladyboy had been enlightening, when it came to sex Dick still preferred the ladies. Nonetheless, the pair still drank together from time to time, each of them finding the other's company to be stimulating. Dick was about to dismiss the beggar from his thoughts but there was something oddly familiar about the man with no legs.

"I think you two have already met," Gemini announced while pointing the beggar out to Fitswell. The man on wheels was only one of a handful of men and street urchins who had suddenly descended on the bar to sell a variety of items from flowers, watches and little flashlights to pirated movie DVD's, cheap shoes and dresses for the bar girls.

"Have we?" asked Fitswell.

"Yes, we have," the beggar announced. "Right now I appear to you as a paraplegic on a skateboard, but you will remember me from long ago in a railroad car."

Dick Fitswell scratched his head, trying to put it together where he had met the beggar, when the beggar spoke up again.

"I'm Harry. But you might remember me better as God."

"Oh course I remember," Dick Fitswell replied as his eventful meeting with God came back to him. "But how do you know Gemini here?"

"He is my messenger," Harry replied. "I needed him to steer you over to Soi Six."

"Is this true?" Dick asked the ladyboy.

"Yes. I am many things, the ladyboy replied. Some people might even call me an angel."

"Well, what I want to know is when I had sex with you was I having sex with a man or a woman?"

"You have probably read that Angels don't have any sexual identity one way or the other so I can be whatever I want to be," Gemini replied.

"The main thing is it doens't really matter," Harry added. "What does matter is that you now have your own place from which you can deliver my message to the world."

"Which is what?" Fitswell asked.

"If you remember I strongly suggested that you spread yourself around more and you haven't let me down in that respect. Meanwhile you have been searching for the perfect fit and when you found her you lost her in that fire in the church. But now you have found your Holy Grail. You just haven't realized it yet."

"I don't understand," said Dick Fitswell.

"You have found something much better than the perfect fit. What you have found is the fountain of youth."

"No I haven't," Dick replied while feeling his face which was covered with a short grey stubble from not shaving. I have too many grey hairs now which proves I am not getting any younger."

"And you won't," said Harry. "But there is this old saying that a man is only as old as the woman he feels."

"Now you have really lost me," Dick replied.

"Think of the situation you have gotten yourself into," said Harry. You have your own bar on Soi Six which is the best street there is in Pattaya which has the finest selection of beatiful women in the entire world. Now if you had a steady girlfriend and even if she was the perfect fit she'd be getting old on you and it wouldn't be very long and she'd no longer be what you once thought she was. But now you have an endless supply of women. And the crop is constantly changing. You can go from bar to bar and have four different girls a day, even more, if you are up to it. And at just 500 baht for each time you have sex that's only sixty bucks for four different women. What you have found is the fountain of youth. But it's for you. It's all yours---this endless supply of an infinite variety of beautiful girls."

"But you really don't need your own bar to enjoy all of that," Gemini added. "But Harry here, he's got a reason for your having that bar and that's why I picked you up on the beach and had sex with you in the first place."

"So what is the purpose of my owning the bar?" Fitswell asked. "And what is it you want me to do?"

"I want you to get your bar on the internet and then I want you to spread the word and to keep spreading it," said Harry.

"And what's that?"

"That you have found the right path for man to follow. And the fountain of eternal youth. You just keep spreading that message and men will keep coming to you in ever increasing numbers. You do that, and I'll take care of the rest."

"Such as?"

"Such as paying off the Thai cops for one thing. I'll make sure that they never close you down, and i'll make sure that your landlord will always be willing to renew your lease. Now let me ask you a final question."

"Go ahead."

"How many big dicks do you have on display right now in your display behind the bar?"

200

"I have twelve. But why are you asking?"

"Then you have 12 to start with to help you spread the word about your Garden of Eden."

"Why are you putting such emphasis on that?" Dick asked.

"I think it's obvious, Dick, if not now, it will be later. But be sure, that number will increase in time."

"So is that all there is to it?"

"That's all," said Harry. "After all, there is nothing more important than man's eternal quest for his holy grail. And that is sex and don't let anyone ever tell you differently. So on that note Gemini and I are going to leave you, but don't worry, we will stay in touch."

For a moment Dick looked down at his beer glass. When he looked up, both were gone.